WALLAND

WALLAND

A NOVEL BY
ANDREA THOME

hesse
creek
media

Published by Hesse Creek Media, Chicago
www.andreathome.net

Edited and Designed by Girl Friday Productions
www.girlfridayproductions.com

Copyediting: Michelle Hope Anderson
Cover Design: Agus Budi Yono
Image Credits: Cover © Andrea Thome, author photo © Terri Carrick

ISBN-13: 9780997850406
e-ISBN: 9780997850413

First Edition

Printed in the United States of America

For Jim, Lila, Landon, and Dad. Thank you for all your love and support. You are my everything. Being a member of your family is the best job I've ever had.

To my close friends who took the time to read and re-read for me: your friendship is treasured. Lisa, Terri, Paula, Lekshmi, Dawn, Shannon, Erin, and my dear, sweet Mim. I couldn't have done it without your constant support along the way.

To the tireless team at Girl Friday—every budding author should treat themselves to the leadership you provide. Thank you for making the process of self-publishing so much simpler . . . and even a little fun.

And to my Mom. Thank you for the writer's gene. And for the strong moral compass. And for teaching me about compassion. And for everything. I miss you.

CHAPTER
ONE

India Evans fiddled with the necklace at her throat as the wheels tucked themselves up into the belly of the plane and the nose shot skyward, up and away from LaGuardia. Spring snowstorms were not unusual in the Northeast, but this one had been unexpected. Forecasters had called for a dusting, and instead Manhattan had awoken to a thick, fluffy blanket of flight delays. It was beautiful, although a little less so on a travel day.

India would have changed her flight if it had been possible, but rescheduling was not an option this time. Jules was flying out of Ohio in a few hours to meet her, and India knew her friend had stretched herself to make this last-minute trip happen.

Julia Haupt had been India's college roommate, and she was still the keeper of all her secrets and basically her favorite person on the planet. India wouldn't risk stranding Jules in a strange city, especially when Julia was dropping everything to join her with almost no notice. Besides, it might have been snowing in New York and Cleveland, but a short flight south to Knoxville, Tennessee, meant landing in springtime temperatures and sunshine. Time to take her homeopathic anxiety remedy and suck it up.

Her fear of flying was one of many recent life developments. It began when India and her fiancé, Jack Sterling, were headed home from their engagement trip to London last fall, having just enjoyed a stopover weekend in Iceland. The landscape of the island nation was spectacular, something out of a Tolkien novel, all sharp peaks and icy valleys. India had thought at the time that Iceland's varied terrain was as different as she and Jack were. She'd spent the weekend traveling around the island, taking the most incredible pictures of the pristine scenery, while Jack had relaxed in the hotel spa, his phone never far from reach.

India had just settled in with her laptop on the flight back, and was beginning to edit her photographs, when the plane had suddenly groaned, followed by a loud popping noise, as masks spilled forth from the overhead panels. Everything shuddered, and the flight attendants scrambled to their jump seats to buckle in. India's initial shock had turned to utter horror when the pilots informed the passengers that they had depressurized and were in an emergency, instructing them to don the oxygen masks at once.

She'd instinctively turned to Jack for comfort, only to discover that he'd been using that moment to Send. Out. A. Tweet. A farewell message to his faithful followers in case he didn't make it. Jack was nothing if not connected. Fortunately, the pilots were able to stabilize at a lower altitude, and a short time later, after maintaining ten thousand feet for a while, they had landed the plane safely at the nearest airport in Nova Scotia.

India was grateful to be alive, but something had shifted inside her. Where there once was the newborn seed of a life with Jack, there now bloomed a sprout of discontent and reservation. The resulting weed was a fast-growing varietal.

She couldn't believe she was engaged to marry someone who could be so narcissistic.

Jack had been chief meteorologist at *Good Morning America* for more than a decade. He was known around town as a bit of a ladies' man but enjoyed the reputation of a gentleman nonetheless. When India was first hired at NBC, she'd received a stunning bouquet of yellow roses from Jack on her second day at work, with a note welcoming India to the big time. Not a bad first impression. India had called over to ABC to thank him, and after exchanging a few flirty e-mails and phone calls over the next several weeks, they'd made plans to meet in person at an annual fund-raising event at a restaurant in Central Park.

It was an unseasonably warm March evening. Jack was hard to resist in his slim-fitted suit, with his golfers' tan and easy smile. Tall, dark, and handsome, with a confidence just on the right side of cocky. At ten years India's senior, he had the air of a man in complete control of his life.

India hadn't pulled any punches getting ready for that first date. She'd tamed her long wavy blonde hair into a side braid, and had chosen to wear the sexy nude pumps she'd been saving for just such an occasion. Her favorite little black dress and Cartier perfume had completed the look. India had played tennis in college, which had done her figure justice in the years since. Jack would later tell her that her confidence and naked ambition were what had sealed the deal. That he knew he'd met his match.

She'd graduated from Vanderbilt at the top of her class and had immediately landed a job in a top-ten market. India had thought she'd be married to her career in her twenties, and had steeled herself for an epic climb. It had to be that way, if she intended to make it to the network before she turned thirty.

India had grown up watching the *Today* show, and she would visualize herself sitting at the anchor desk one day. She was single-minded in her determination, and she had no intention of letting anything, especially a romantic relationship, get in the way of reaching that goal. She'd learned at an early age that family didn't have to be a priority—at least it hadn't been for her parents. The thought of driving kids in a car pool gave her hives.

She enjoyed her position as an anchor on *Weekend Today* and knew she was in a prime position to move up in the ranks, even though she'd only been on the job a few months.

Ratings were robust, and it had quickly become clear that India was a rising star. She was a bit of a media darling, and it wasn't unusual to see pictures of herself at events in the New York papers.

She had been perfectly content to bide her time on the weekend desk, when network executives had suddenly approached her with an opportunity. They'd wanted her to join the weekday team, where she would sit at the anchor desk with the big four. Rather than being named the lead female anchor, however, India would be a third-hour lifestyle anchor, reporting on celebrities and fashion.

How could she say no?

It was so close to the brass ring, and she could cut her teeth waiting for the main anchor chair to eventually open up. The current lead female anchor had recently delivered her third child, so it likely wouldn't be long before she sought the scheduling flexibility that the network magazine shows could provide her.

Station execs also mentioned that they wouldn't mind having the opportunity to feature India's wedding. Viewers had gone nuts when Jack had shown up on the plaza last summer to pop the question during a segment India was hosting. It was no surprise that their engagement had coincided with a ratings period. The bride and groom were both in television, after all. These were things to consider, and her fiancé certainly had.

Theirs was a whirlwind courtship. Jack had plenty of experience in the charm and romance department, and he'd made India feel that she was every bit worth the wait. They'd spent most of the weekends that summer and fall after their engagement out on his boat, the *Court Ship*, learning everything they could about each other. They were rarely alone, though, since Jack's family enjoyed the boat as much as they did, and they were afforded carte blanche access.

His brothers had paraded their numerous girlfriends up and down the docks, day and night, most of them not getting the memo to remove their stilettos before boarding. India was not exactly a shrinking violet; she'd always made friends easily, and she enjoyed many of the colorful women that his brothers played host to. She only wished there were a few more repeat customers. Despite the foot traffic, she'd found herself feeling exceptionally lonely during much of the time she spent with Jack. It was almost as if he had landed his big fish and was now content having it hanging on the wall, for all to see.

They made a striking couple, and the voracious appetite of the tabloids was kept satiated by their busy social schedules. Jack loved the Manhattan scene even more than India did. They were a match made in broadcast heaven, as coworkers and friends constantly reminded them. Colleagues liked to tease India about being cherry-picked; it was as if Jack had placed an order for the perfect wife, and India had arrived right on cue.

She would have preferred a more private proposal, but India knew how happy the attention made her fiancé. It wasn't every day that a competing network's anchor proposed to his girlfriend on live morning television. Of course people would be interested, Jack had reminded her more than once. But as time went on, India felt herself becoming bitter about agreeing to let the audience weigh in on every decision regarding the wedding.

But Jack was so enamored by the idea of the two of them becoming an "it" couple that India held her tongue. Every decision, from the venue to the dress, was met with unsolicited advice on social media. Fortunately, her tall slender frame was flattered by all of the dresses the network selected. Still, India had found herself dreading their wedding day instead of looking forward to it, and she'd watched her fiancé morph into a different person with each passing day.

Jack had rarely asked India's opinion before making decisions that affected them both. He'd chosen the honeymoon spot. He'd hired the wedding coordinator. He'd decided where they would spend the holidays and with whom. In some ways, after having had to depend on herself for most of her life, it was a relief not to have to be in charge.

But that moment on the airplane. She couldn't stop thinking about it. When she'd finally mentioned that it bothered her, Jack had brushed her off, saying he knew they were going to be OK all along and that it was good for their image as a couple to have that kind of social media presence in the midst of such a big news story. He'd told her she shouldn't be so sensitive, that her strength and self-sufficiency were two of the qualities he'd admired most when they'd met. Besides, that tweet had gotten almost a million likes!

The following weeks and months had flown by, and before they knew it, Christmas was over and the wedding day was upon them. But, for India, the discontent that had taken root during their engagement had grown into a full-blown panic. Somehow, she'd thought she could manage to tuck it deep down, beneath the layers of tulle on her custom gown, her least favorite of the four options. She'd felt like she should be spinning inside of a jewelry box. In the eerie quiet of the bride's dressing room, she'd finally acknowledged the sinking feeling she'd been ignoring since the moment she'd said yes. She'd actually meant no. This marriage, like her audience-selected footwear, wasn't the right fit.

There was no way was she was going to be a runaway bride. It was too cliché. Even though she'd known she couldn't marry Jack, she'd respected him enough not to leave him standing alone in front of a church full of people. With a sinking feeling in the pit of her stomach, she'd sent for her fiancé. India had slid back out of her chosen Choos and waited. Listening to the faraway notes of the chamber music filtering through the walls of St. Patrick's, she'd realized that, for the first time ever, she was dreading doing the very thing that she loved most: delivering the news.

Viewers were heartbroken when the morning-show super couple called it quits. India got letters chiding her for jilting the beloved Jack. His sad picture was the only one splashed across the cover of the magazines, and India was sure it had been carefully orchestrated. He'd done a wonderful job of rebounding, though, as evidenced by a more recent photo on

Page Six. He'd been spotted having drinks at a Midtown hotel with a rising celebrity chef on his arm, the media speculating about what Jack might be "cooking up" these days. India was happy and relieved he'd been able to move on so quickly, and she would have told him so, but they hadn't spoken since their nonwedding day.

She'd gone right back to work, refusing to discuss details with anyone, but it was always an elephant in the room. She was obviously professional and more than capable of doing her job, but after the ratings took a dip, station execs had come to her with a suggestion.

They'd offered her a week off, under the condition that she would give them an exclusive interview when she returned: "India and Jack: What Went Wrong?" To them, it was morning-show porn. Personally, India would have rather eaten a box of tacks, but she'd agreed to the interview in an effort to save her job. It was made clear to her that declining the offer was not an option. It was clear they thought that her time away would heal the viewers' wounds and allow India to return and pick up where she'd left off a few weeks before the beginning of the all-important May sweeps. So now she found herself on a plane to Knoxville, to recharge and spend time with her best friend. She'd agreed to management's terms, hoping she could pull it off without feeling like she'd sold her soul to the devil.

CHAPTER
TWO

Once the plane touched down in Knoxville, India felt herself relax a little. She hadn't realized how badly she'd needed to put some physical distance between herself and the whole mess. India considered the upcoming week that she and Julia would spend together. She'd seen a story on Blackberry Farm years ago when she was working in Atlanta, and she'd been impressed enough to make a mental note to visit. It had never dawned on her that it would be as a newly single woman, with miles of uncertainty before her. The resort would be the perfect place to hide out and lick her wounds.

Even though they were the best of friends, India and Julia couldn't have been more different. India liked spontaneity; Julia craved routine. India loved to travel to exotic places and was a bit of a daredevil; Jules was a first-class wife and mother, totally willing to put the needs of her family ahead of her own. Fortunately, the resort had workshops and events that appealed to each of them. India could take classes and go on hikes, and Julia could lose herself in a sea of spa treatments.

They'd lucked out and, thanks to a cancellation, were able to book one of the newest luxury cottages on the property. India was looking forward to breaking in her new camera in the photography workshop she'd signed up for. India had minored in photography at Vanderbilt, but she'd never seemed to have the time to learn how to make the most of her equipment. Now was the perfect opportunity.

The resort in Walland, Tennessee, was only about a thirty-minute drive from Knoxville, and it had a reputation for offering the best of two worlds to the discerning luxury traveler. It was possible to enjoy all the pleasures of field and stream during the day and then sit down to a dinner prepared by a James Beard Award–winning chef, complete with stellar service from one of the resort's renowned sommeliers. If you wanted for anything, the answer was always yes.

India stepped onto the escalator and headed down to baggage claim, switching on her phone to see if Jules's plane had taken off on time. As the phone sprang to life, the pings started and didn't stop. Fourteen text messages later, India had pieced together the news.

Julia wouldn't be coming.

Pearl, her four-year-old daughter, had come down with a brutal combination of the chicken pox and a flu virus. India read through the text messages that chronicled Julia's internal struggle:

Would it be terrible if I left Mike with the kids, and came anyway?

There is just no way I could do it.

Maybe I could come down for the second half of the week?

In the end, it was clear that it just wasn't going to happen. India was going to have to go it alone on this trip.

She felt unexpected tears prick at her eyes, coupled with shame for feeling so needy.

Of course India wouldn't ask Julia to leave her sick child. It was one of the things she loved most about her best friend: she was always there for family and friends, no matter what. India understood why Julia felt so conflicted; her friend knew how badly India needed her shoulder—and ear—right now. But Julia also knew that this time it was her little girl who needed her most.

India had just balled up part of her sleeve to dab at the corners of her eyes when she heard his voice for the very first time.

"Waiting half an hour for luggage makes me want to cry too."

India sniffled, straightening her shoulders and trying to shake off the tears that had snuck up on her so unexpectedly. She turned and found herself looking up at one of the most ruggedly beautiful human beings she'd ever seen. Thick dark curls peeked out from under his ball cap, and a half smile produced a dimple she instinctively wanted to put her finger in. But that voice. The hair on her neck stood up as she tried to speak.

"Oh right. It does seem to be taking a long time." She blinked rapidly, trying to regain her composure. "I think I have something in my eye."

What was that? It was the best she could do with those whiskey-colored eyes examining her so closely. She waited for to him to speak again.

"Allergies this time of year can be something," he said over his shoulder as he walked a few steps to a nearby coffee kiosk and grabbed a handful of napkins. He returned and handed them to her, watching her as she dabbed at her eyes. "Is this your first time in Knoxville?"

India tried to remind herself to breathe. Was the air thinner in Knoxville? Why had it suddenly become so warm in the terminal? She reached up and fingered her necklace nervously with her free hand, watching him closely.

"Yes, first time," she said, admiring the hands that had just handed her the napkins, her tears already forgotten.

She realized she shouldn't be wasting time staring at his massive hands when there were so many other things to take in. But she couldn't help herself. She had a flash of all the things he could do with them, and instantly felt the blush rise up from her neck to her cheeks.

"I'm so sorry, I seem to be having some kind of reaction to something. It's awfully warm in here, isn't it?"

Wyatt Hinch had hardly moved a muscle. He stood rooted in place, fixated on this beguiling woman who couldn't seem to get herself together. The luggage belt sprang to life with a buzzer so loud, she jumped and involuntarily inched another step closer to him.

He caught the scent of her.

Springtime.

He surprised himself with that. It had been so long since he'd let a woman close enough to be in any way affected. But this woman was struggling, and the least he could do was be a gentleman. He watched her prepare to grab her duffel. "Here, let me help," he offered as he brushed by her to lift it off the belt himself. "Whoa. It must not be a short trip," he added as the bag came to a rest with a soft thump at her feet.

As if his hands weren't enough, the flexing of those forearms as he lifted her bag off the belt was almost more than India could take. It took physical effort not to swoon.

"Oh, thank you. You didn't have to do that."

Calm down, India, she thought, annoyed with herself for feeling more flustered than usual.

"Of course," he said with a smile. "Enjoy your trip."

Handsome and kind. It was like seeing a unicorn. India did her best to breathe normally as he turned away from her to watch for his own bag.

She pulled up her luggage handle, and she was about to head outside when her phone started ringing. She fumbled to find it in the bottom of her purse and answered just before it went to voice mail. It was Julia.

"Oh my God, I'm so sorry! I am totally failing you as a friend in your hour of need. I should just tell Mike that he can handle this and get my ass to the airport, shouldn't I? Are you OK? How was the flight? Did the snow this morning make you crazy? I stalked you with the Find My Friends app, so I knew you were already there."

Julia prattled on, obviously still feeling guilty about her decision to stay home with the baby. It was clear she was working on very little sleep and copious amounts of dark-roast coffee. India tried to put her mind at ease, telling Julia that it was fine, and that if she had to be alone for a week, Blackberry Farm wasn't a terrible place to be stranded.

"It's OK, Jules. You're a sweetheart for feeling so guilty, but your family needs you. Besides, that's why God invented FaceTime. Just promise me when you finally get everyone to sleep, and the puking stops, you'll crawl into a bottle of wine and call me."

"Promise. It's a date. Love you, friend. Take care of yourself this week. And find some hot ranch hand to have your way with, OK?"

Instinctively, India glanced over her shoulder and saw that the man who'd helped her with her bag was watching her. A blush betrayed her again. Damn it. There had to be a laser treatment to solve that problem. Making a mental note to call her dermatologist the minute she got home, she smiled weakly, and answered, "OK, Jules. I'll get right on that."

"That's what she said, heh-heh. Talk later."

India hung up and started to gather her luggage and purse. With one last look at the man, she smiled.

"Thanks again. I appreciate the kindness."

He had retrieved his own bag now, and he started walking away from the baggage claim alongside India.

"I couldn't help but overhearing that you're going to Blackberry Farm. I'm actually headed that way myself. I'm happy to give you a lift if you haven't made other arrangements?"

What the hell was he doing? The words came out before he realized what he was saying. But there was that blush again, creeping across her chest and onto her cheeks. He smiled in spite of himself. It felt good to know he still had it.

It had been way too long since he'd even thought about flirting with someone. Besides, this was a harmless offer. He would drop her at the farm, and she would disappear into the flowers and fauna for the week. He probably wouldn't see her again.

Harmless flirting felt safe.

And, damn, it felt good.

"Oh, I have a rental car," India said. "Wait. I actually don't. I mean, I did."

Spit it out, India, she thought.

"My friend was supposed to meet me, and she had the rental car lined up. She had to cancel, so I guess now I technically don't have a ride. Are you sure you wouldn't mind? I promise not to babble the entire way."

"No problem. You probably won't want to leave the property once you're there anyway. A car is kind of a waste. Why don't you wait, and I'll run out to the lot and swing around to meet you here. I'll be in a green pickup."

Of course he drove a truck. There was no way this man folded himself into a fussy luxury car. India watched, along with several other female passengers, as he hustled across the passenger lanes and then disappeared into the long-term parking garage. He was almost as good-looking from behind.

She was a little surprised at herself for accepting a ride from a total stranger, but she was banking on the fact that someone kind enough to help her out in a moment of need wouldn't turn out to be a total psycho.

CHAPTER
THREE

Wyatt climbed into the old green truck he'd affectionately named Olive and fired up the engine. "Uncle John's Band" filtered out of the speakers, making him smile. Now that he was back in Tennessee, he felt himself relax a little, the energy of his home turf loosening his bones and easing his spirit. He loved to travel, especially when it was for work.

He'd been freelancing as a photographer for *National Geographic* for the past decade, and the work fed his soul like nothing else. The thrill of capturing the perfect shot never got old, whether it was a sweeping snap of a mountain range in Washington State or the craggy face of a Buddhist monk in Nepal. That instant his finger made contact with the button and captured a moment in time was *it* for him. Such a rush.

He'd always loved taking pictures. His mother had insisted that her son be well rounded, not solely focused on sports and brawn. While he loved the satisfaction he got from heavy labor on the farm growing up, he was also encouraged by his parents to explore other pursuits. Wyatt had participated in a photography camp one summer in high school, and he'd been instantly hooked. He'd saved every penny to invest in some high-quality equipment, which he'd fooled around with on his own. But those camps were really where he'd cut his teeth. The young woman who ran them, Violet, was then a recent graduate from the Rocky Mountain School of Photography, and her passion for the outdoors was evident in the way she taught.

Now, years later, he sometimes partnered with Violet and her husband, Rex, to shoot marketing materials for Blackberry Farm. They had become the best of friends, and Violet and Rex had seen Wyatt through the darkest time of his life. They'd been there when he and Claire had attended that final summer camp. They'd witnessed the love that had bloomed between them—the wild, unbridled passion of young lovers getting their first taste.

And they'd been there when Claire had gotten sick.

Even now, the thought of seeing his old friends after two months away put a smile on his face. He wondered what they would think if they saw him showing up with a beautiful woman in the passenger seat. He shook his head at the thought. Better not let Violet get a sniff of that, or she'd try to play matchmaker. She'd have him married off if it were the last thing she ever accomplished.

As he rounded a curve, he could see her up ahead, waiting where he'd left her on the sidewalk. To say she was striking would be an understatement. She was simply one of the most naturally beautiful women he had ever seen. She had to be five ten, because, at six three, he didn't tower over her the way he did with most women. And he'd only helped her with her bag as a courtesy; she was athletic and looked more than capable of handling it herself.

It was more than her physical beauty that was mesmerizing. She was an interesting combination of confidence and a seeming lack of self-awareness. It was the sadness in those clear blue eyes, though, that had drawn him to her in the airport, encouraging him to offer his help. Her expression betrayed a vulnerability. She was wounded, and the part of him that was also damaged wanted to know why.

Jesus. He was just giving her a ride. No need to make a *Movie of the Week* out of this. He unconsciously shook his head as he eased his old truck up to the curb. Jumping out, he hustled around to interrupt her efforts to drag her own bag into the bed of his truck.

"Here, please, let me. Although I don't doubt you're capable, this baby isn't exactly a featherweight."

He grabbed the handle and effortlessly swung the duffel into Olive's backseat.

"Besides, you never know when rain could surprise us. East Tennessee weather can be a little unpredictable. Better to keep it back here to be on the safe side."

He set her shoulder bag next to her duffel on the backseat and then stepped toward the passenger door to open it for her.

India had been trying not to stand there watching him like some slack-jawed imbecile, but she was fighting a losing battle. This man was an uncommon find, to say the least. She felt herself smile a little at his suggestion of her capability. It was something she wasn't used to with Jack. He had always been the perfect gentleman, but he'd also managed to make her feel like a helpless weakling, which she most certainly was not. It felt good to witness chivalry on her behalf, while not feeling like she was less-than for accepting the help.

"Thanks. I didn't consider that. I do have some equipment in that carry-on that I'd rather not get wet."

India pivoted toward the open passenger door and climbed into the truck. She was instantly intoxicated by the smell of leather and something else. What was it? Burning leaves? Tobacco? Whatever it was, the interior of this truck smelled like he looked.

She could tell he'd had the truck for some time by the scattered hints of comfortable ownership. There were coins and a pack of gum in the cup holder. A pair of aviator glasses hung from the rearview mirror, and a small photo of a little girl with ringlets was tucked against the dash. The seats were worn in and inviting, the vehicle almost as appealing to her as the man who drove it. This truck was clearly loved.

She startled as he jerked open his door and swung himself into the driver's seat. He started up the engine and brought the truck to life.

"This old girl might be well worn, but she'll get us to where we're going. My friends were kind enough to drop her off at the airport for me, so I'd have a familiar face to come home to. I've been gone awhile, so it's nice to get home to Olive."

So he was married. Damn. He wasn't wearing a ring, so she'd been sure he wasn't. She frowned slightly, suddenly despising someone she had never met.

"Will Olive mind that you're giving me a ride? It's not too late for me to jump in a cab."

He chuckled under his breath.

"I hope she doesn't mind, since you're sitting in her. Olive is my truck. She's the familiar face I'm happy to see. This truck has been my partner for a dozen or so years. She's pretty understanding, and she's not the jealous type."

There was that blush again. He could get used to that, if only because it told him he was having some effect on her.

"Oh, OK. It's a cool truck. I can tell you've had it for a while."

He gave her a sideways glance, and crooked his eyebrow in question as he eased onto the highway. India felt her stomach flutter.

"I mean that as a compliment! It's obvious that the two of you are comfortable with each other," she said.

She watched as the concrete buildings of the airport gave way to the verdant green landscape along the Lamar Alexander Parkway. She felt herself relax a little, but she was still aware of the electricity crackling between them. She realized she hadn't introduced herself yet.

"I'm India, by the way. It's strange—I know the name of your truck, and I haven't had the good manners to introduce myself." She smiled. "I really appreciate the ride."

He smiled back at her, nodding his head.

"I'm Wyatt. And it's my pleasure. What brings you to town?"

He noticed her shift in her seat and saw the shadows flicker briefly in her eyes. She didn't let them linger, though. He sensed her need to show strength again, like she'd tried to do back in the terminal, and he made a note of it.

"I was supposed to meet my best friend for a photography workshop and wellness week, but her daughter got sick, so now I'm solo. It's OK. I'm happy to have the peace and quiet and the chance to regroup."

The words slipped out before she could stop them.

"What are you regrouping from? If you don't mind me asking. If you do, just say so. I won't be offended."

Wyatt could tell that she wouldn't go into great detail, but it felt rude not to ask when she had offered the reason for her visit so freely.

She took a breath and decided to be honest. She wouldn't see him again after this, and it would feel good to talk to someone about the whole situation, especially since she wouldn't get to break it down with Julia this week.

"I'm taking some time off from my job to reassess my life," India offered. "And when you work in Manhattan, you want to get as far away from civilization as you can. Turns out . . . people are overrated."

She gave him a sheepish smile and shrugged her shoulders.

"Have you ever had a plan in place, and then, all of a sudden, felt like the rug got pulled out from under you? Yeah. So that happened, and I guess now I have to come to terms with it. The trouble is, I'm not sure where to go from here. I'm not used to feeling so lost."

He was quiet. The silence was deafening, so she stole a glance at him, and noticed his jaw was locked and he looked a little pale. It was a moment or two before he spoke.

"Yeah, I've had the rug pulled out from under me before. Plan B can be tough to figure out. I'm still working on it."

He sighed, clearly troubled by something.

"You're coming to the right place, though," he informed her with forced cheer. "The farm is peaceful, and the photography seminar you mentioned is great. My friends are the teachers, actually. People come back year after year to build on what they've learned. And there is no better place to get lost with your camera and your thoughts."

He knew he was rambling and did his best to stop.

"So that's the equipment you wanted to keep dry, I'm assuming?" he asked.

He tried to relax his grip on the steering wheel. Way to masterfully change the subject. Smooth as silk.

It was clear to India that he didn't want to hear about her personal drama and was politely trying to steer the conversation elsewhere. She forged ahead.

"Yeah, photography is kind of a passion of mine. I studied it back in college, even thought I might pursue it after graduation, but it wasn't in the cards. This seemed like a good opportunity to revisit it, since I have some unexpected free time now."

That was better. Talk about something safe until they reached the farm and she could get the heck out of his truck without embarrassing herself any further. It was clear he had no idea who she was, and she wanted to keep it that way. She'd had enough public humiliation to last a lifetime. She'd be surprised if this man even owned a television. He seemed too smart for that.

"Your friends are the teachers?" India asked. "I seem to remember reading that the female instructor has a knack for still-life photography. I think the brochure said that she studied out in the Rockies somewhere?"

His easy smile returned. It was clear he held his friends in high regard.

"Violet is one of the best. She and Rex met while they were students at school in Missoula. They used to teach a youth camp here in the summers, which is where I met them years ago. Violet pretty much taught me everything I know. You'll love them both."

So he was a fellow photography enthusiast. She was about to ask him about it, when he adjusted the knob on the radio, and the strains of a U2 song filled the truck. She took the hint and sat back to enjoy the view.

Wyatt slowed the truck a few minutes later, turning right onto West Millers Cove Road. As the truck rolled up and over a gentle slope in the road, Bono was singing about still not finding what he was looking for, and the signature white split-rail fence that flanked the meadows came into view.

"There it is. One of the most beautiful places on earth. I'm jealous that you're getting to experience it for the first time, although returning here really never gets old."

Wyatt flashed her a grin and then rolled the windows down, as if to inch closer to this place that was clearly special to him.

"I'll drop you off at reception and they'll check you in and run you to your room. Do you know where you're staying?"

India smiled. "I lucked out and got one of the new cottages that overlook the garden. It sounds pretty incredible."

India locked eyes with him briefly.

"And like a photographer's dream spot," she added.

"For sure. You won't be disappointed."

Wyatt maneuvered the truck under the portico outside reception. He was out of his seat and around to her door before she knew what was happening. He helped her climb out of the cab as the bellman approached.

"Well, look who's back. Welcome home, Wyatt. How was your trip?"

The tall russet-haired man who'd joined them to help with India's bags had a huge smile on his handsome face. He nodded his head to India.

"Welcome to Blackberry Farm, ma'am."

He turned his attention back to Wyatt, offering his hand in greeting.

Wyatt seemed to be well known and admired, as other members of the team joined them to say hello. India figured he must be a frequent visitor, which was odd, considering he was local.

"Hey, Garrett, good to see you, buddy. Been way too long. Let's catch up over a beer this week."

Wyatt asked Garrett to help with the luggage, then returned his attention to India. Their eyes met again, and he watched the pink of her cheeks reward him one final time. The effect rendered him speechless.

"Well, thanks again," she said, breaking the silence. "It was really nice of you to give me a lift. I guess you can scratch that good deed off your list for the day," she said, happy to be rewarded once more with his incredible smile. "It was nice to meet you, Wyatt. And thanks to Olive too. She's a beauty."

Wyatt took her hand in his, and he couldn't help but notice the rise of panic that he felt at the thought of not seeing her again.

"My pleasure, really. Enjoy your time here. I hope it brings you the peace you're looking for."

He reluctantly let go of her hand, forcing himself to ignore the current between them.

"It's a good place to contemplate your plan B," he added with an almost imperceptible wink. He jumped back into his truck and drove away, leaving India on the stone drive smiling to herself.

CHAPTER
FOUR

India completed the check-in process, stopping by the concierge desk to get an updated list of activities. Looking over her itinerary for the workshop, she noticed there was a welcome dinner out at the Yallerhammer Pavilion scheduled for that evening. She'd wait and see if she felt up to it; it might be easier to throw on her pajamas and hunker down in front of the fireplace. Besides, she'd already done a thorough job of embarrassing herself at the airport. Maybe she wasn't ready to participate in a group activity quite yet.

She joined Garrett in one of the farm's signature SUVs, which was already loaded with her luggage. The gravel crunched under the tires as they drove back out through the front gate and down the fenced lane toward her cottage. Garrett filled her in on some details about the farm. He pointed out the dairy, where they made their own cheeses, which was next to the brewery. Her cottage was close to the barn, where formal dinners were held in the evenings. India marveled at the size of the farm.

"This place is bigger than I thought. How many acres is it?"

Garrett pulled up to a set of white gates that opened automatically when he pushed a remote.

"Blackberry itself covers about forty-two hundred acres, but there's a sister property down the road that has another five thousand. It's been owned by the same family for over forty years now."

He stole a shy glance at her, a smile blooming from underneath his short goatee.

"Are you a friend of Wyatt's?" he asked.

India looked puzzled at first, but she answered smoothly. "No, we met at the airport—he heard I was headed here and offered me a lift. You know him well?"

She knew he must by the expression on his face. She figured she might as well go fishing for a little more information, and Garrett was more than happy to provide.

"Oh, everyone loves Wyatt. He makes you feel like you've known him forever, even those of us who are newer to the area, like myself."

He grinned.

"I recently relocated from Washington State. My family owned a farm there, so I was hoping to get a job working in gardens, but when the opportunity to work here became available, I jumped at the chance. Carrying bags is honest work, but digging in the dirt is my real passion."

He guided the car into a gravel drive, which led to the most charming collection of structures India had ever seen. "Here we are: the Garden Cottages. That's the main house there." He gestured to a large wooden home filled with picture windows up on the top of a hill.

"That little stone cottage next to it is called Root Cellar. And this one here is yours; we call it Woodshed."

She admired the red-sided building; noticing the sloping tin roof, she hoped she'd get to hear rain patter against it at least once. Her cottage was down below the other two, closest to the gardens, offering generous views from a screened-in porch.

"You must really be lucky," Garrett continued. "The wait list for these places is a mile long, and they used to only rent them out together for groups."

He offered his hand, helping her out of the car.

"I'll take you in and show you around before I bring in your luggage, just to make sure it suits your needs."

He smiled at her.

"Although I can't imagine you won't fall in love with it. Everyone does."

Garrett used the key to unlock the farmhouse door and then swung it open, while India stood behind him on the path, taking in the breathtaking landscape before her. There was nothing but gardens as far as the eye could see. It was obvious that some of the rows were still being prepared for plantings, while other winter and early-spring foods had already begun to poke up from the ground, dotting the fields with pops of green.

Further evidence of the busy season were the sacks of soil stacked around the gardens and the bustle of activity outside of a planting shed, which was about five hundred feet from her front porch. Shielding her eyes from the sun, she could make out an older gentleman in overalls talking to another man with his broad back to her. They were gesturing animatedly over a rudimentary table filled with seedlings.

"OK, right this way."

Garrett turned and followed her gaze, breaking into a huge grin.

"That's Finn Janssen. He's our master gardener. He might look like a simple country man, but don't be fooled. That fellow there knows more about heirloom farming and sustainable growing than most folks you'll meet. Everything that comes out of these gardens ends up in the kitchens at Blackberry. You've never tasted food so delicious in your life."

India stood watching them. The men were clearly engrossed in what they were discussing.

"I've read about Mr. Janssen," she said. "He sounds like he has a real passion for what he does. I'm grateful that there are still farmers around who want to protect the integrity of our food."

Garrett raised his eyebrows, impressed. "My grandparents never farmed any other way. I'd give anything to work with him someday. He's a real pioneer in the industry. Make sure you get over to meet him sometime this week if you can."

India pointed to the small red building where the farmer worked.

"I definitely want to take a peek at his shed, and maybe even photograph him working, since they're obviously getting ready to put the rest of the crops in."

Garrett nodded in agreement. "Yep. Finn is a good and kind man, and smarter than most. I'm sure he would welcome the chance to share his love of food from the source."

Garrett raised his hand to wave at Finn, who had turned around and was looking their way, as if sensing he was being discussed. Finn nodded back and smiled in their direction, raising his hand in greeting. At that moment, India realized who the farmer had been talking to.

Wyatt pivoted toward them, offering a smile and a sheepish wave, before turning his attention back to Finn. Her stomach clenched at the unexpected sight of him. He was probably just saying hello to friends while he was in the area. She shouldn't be that surprised to see him. But she wasn't disappointed either.

Garrett subtly gestured to get her attention. "C'mon, let's get you settled in."

With that, he motioned for her to cross the threshold into the cottage.

If the landscape outside had been sweeping and widespread, the inside of this charming space was just the opposite. She felt as if she were being hugged by her surroundings. It was the perfect mix of reclaimed wood and beefy old stones, which surrounded a massive fireplace on the far wall. There was an overstuffed sofa in front of the hearth, and a table filled with *Town & Country* and *Field & Stream* magazines. The lingering aroma of a recent fire prickled her nose in the best possible way. It smelled like the woods. It smelled like Wyatt.

She started at the thought. What was it about that man that had infected her thoughts? She wasn't looking for romance while she was here, despite Julia's teasing. She'd learned her lesson in that department.

She turned back toward Garrett, who was waiting expectantly for her approval.

"It's pretty great, huh?" he said. "It's totally different than the other two Garden Cottages, but they're all favorites of our guests. You have another view of Root Cellar through there."

He gestured toward an antique glass window on the west wall.

She moved toward the sill and peered out, spotting the small building again, now a hundred or so feet away, up on a cliff. It couldn't look more different from her cottage with its stone exterior and charming slate roof. Garrett was right. She was in love.

"It's perfect. Thanks, Garrett. They're lucky to have you here; you're a great ambassador for the farm."

He thanked her with a quiet smile and then moved toward the door. India poked around her temporary home while he went out to fetch her bags from the car. Once her things were inside and she'd said good-bye, she kicked her shoes off, climbed up onto the most exquisitely furnished king-size bed, and promptly fell fast asleep.

"Don't look. I'm serious, Finn. Don't!" Wyatt felt like a teenager, but he didn't want her to think he was a stalker. Finn completely ignored the plea and took great pleasure in slowly turning his gaze toward Woodshed. He lifted his hand and smiled at the twosome standing on the porch.

"I see what's got you all bunched up. She's a fine-looking lass," he said as he turned his attention back to Wyatt. "Why don't you ask her to supper in the barn?"

Wyatt glanced over his shoulder and saw the recognition cross her face when she realized it was him. She was even more lovely standing with her hand over her eyes, bathed in the late-afternoon sunlight. He felt an unfamiliar tightening in his chest, which made him uncomfortable. He offered her a meek smile and halfheartedly waved back.

"Great. Now she thinks I'm some psycho," he said through clenched teeth as Finn laughed at him.

Wyatt blew out the breath he hadn't realized he'd been holding.

"And I'm not asking her to dinner. It was a simple ride from the airport. I don't even know why I told you about it."

Finn turned around and threw his hands up, tired of hearing Wyatt's excuses.

"Finn, don't start. You're starting to sound like Violet."

Wyatt exhaled and busied his hands rearranging the contents of the table.

Finn had known Wyatt since he was a child. He knew when to push and when not to. Wyatt had experienced his share of sadness, and Finn would never want to see the boy hurt that way again. But there was living to do, and Finn had sensed something different in Wyatt's eyes when he'd relayed the story of this morning to him. There was a spark he hadn't seen there since, well . . . since Claire. He shuddered to think about how losing her had left Wyatt a shell of a person for so long. It was time for him to heal.

Finn followed his instinct to push back this time.

"Don't get ornery with me, son. I know you better than you know yourself. You're intrigued. All I'm saying is, don't close yourself off to the possibility of something. You might just wait too long, and the opportunities will dry up, along with your good looks."

Finn rolled his eyes when Wyatt cracked a grin.

When Finn spoke next, his voice was choked with emotion. "You deserve to be happy, Wyatt. And that damned career of yours sure won't keep you warm at night."

They locked eyes, and Finn raised his brow in defiance.

Wyatt couldn't help but chuckle. He knew Finn meant well. Hell, if anyone understood him, it was the old farmer. Finn had lived alone for a long time, having lost his wife in their first year of marriage during childbirth. He'd never remarried, but he'd always seemed fulfilled by his role at the farm. Wyatt wondered now if that wasn't the case after all.

"I appreciate that you're worried about me, but I can take care of myself. Just like you have. Anyway, I want to relax this time while I'm home. Take in the change of the seasons and shoot some landscape stuff." Finn nodded in agreement as

Wyatt continued. "Speaking of, do you know where they put Violet and Rex up for the week? I'm assuming they brought Sadie with them?"

Finn snickered at the mention of the little girl. "Oh yeah, little miss is here with them, and boy is she something. Last time she was in the gardens, she had me out here pushing her around in the wheelbarrow until I thought I was gonna drop. They're staying in the farmhouse this time, and I think I just saw them pull up a little while ago from their afternoon of fishing, so you should be in luck if you wanna say hey."

The men grabbed each other in a brief embrace, promising to see each other later. Finn disappeared into his shed while Wyatt headed back to his truck and pointed her in the direction of the farmhouse.

It was good to be home again.

He had originally planned to stay away another month, but as the years went by, he'd found himself less and less interested in prolonged absences from this place. Sure, the travel scratched an itch, but his true satisfaction these days was in returning home to share his adventures with family and friends.

Showing his work to Violet had always made him proud, especially since she'd been the catalyst for him getting the job in the first place. One of her friends from photography school in Missoula was a photo editor at *National Geographic*, so she'd made a phone call on Wyatt's behalf that had changed— and arguably saved—his life.

He'd been lost, heartbroken, and not sure how to be alone after he'd been a part of something so all-encompassing. Violet knew what Claire had meant to him, but she also knew that his love of photography could be a buoy for Wyatt when he so desperately needed one. She didn't hesitate, knowing that when *National Geographic* saw Wyatt's work, they would hire him on the spot. She wasn't wrong on either account.

Now, all these years later, Wyatt knew that Violet and Rex were more than friends to him. They were part of his family.

His chosen family.

The thought made him smile as he threw the truck into park outside the farmhouse. He could hardly wait to get inside.

CHAPTER
FIVE

The chirping of her cell phone roused India from her nap, and she flopped her hand around on the bed, searching for the damned thing. The bright afternoon light had been replaced by the angled rays of the setting sun, bathing her room in a soft hazy light. As she lifted the phone to her ear, she could already hear Jules's voice calling her name.

"India? Did I wake you? I can't believe you were taking a nap. You don't take naps! Now I'm really worried. Are you depressed? Do I need to FedEx you some Xanax?"

Julia finally took a breath, allowing India a moment to respond.

"I'm fine, Jules. I must've dozed off for a minute. I won't let it happen again."

India yawned and stretched, sinking her long frame deeper into the down coverlet. The thought occurred to her that she could easily stay right here for the entire week, if she wanted to.

Julia sighed, relieved. That was the India she knew and loved. She believed her friend would make it through this rough patch, but she wished she were there with her to help move the process along in person.

"How was the trip from the airport? I totally forgot to remind you about the rental car! Did you have any trouble getting one?"

That was Julia. A puking, pockmarked child at home, and she was still going over the mental checklist to make sure her friend was OK.

"Actually, I got a ride from a guy I met in baggage claim who was headed this way. He was super handsome, so I took him up on his offer of a lift."

India flopped back against her pillow and waited for the reaction. She smiled in anticipation.

"*What?* Oh my God . . . *you* hitchhiked? You won't even use Uber! Are you crazy? What if he was some lunatic who recognized you, then whisked you away, and chopped you into bits? Why would you do that? I knew you weren't thinking clearly. I'm coming down there."

India couldn't help herself. She burst out laughing, loving her best friend even more in that moment. The perfect yin to her yang.

"I'm fine, and you know I wouldn't have accepted if I hadn't checked him out and decided he was totally normal. And, Jules . . ." She paused, conjuring up the image of him, which wasn't hard, considering he'd filled her naptime dreams. "He was really, really hot. I mean, like, super hot. He was nice too . . . but mostly hot."

Julia was cracking up now.

"It seems like he knows everyone here at Blackberry," India continued. "He must have grown up with the family that owns it or something."

Julia sighed dramatically, but her tone was teasing now. "When I told you to find a plaything, I guess I didn't expect you to start trolling for men at the airport. But, hey, I'm glad he did it for you. Wait. Where is he now? Are you alone?"

India giggled. "Are you seriously asking me if I brought him back here to have my way with him? Please. It was all very proper. He dropped me off at reception, and that was that. It was a harmless flirtation. Get ahold of yourself!" Julia laughed as India continued. "Might I recommend a trip to Walgreens? It sounds like you really need to get out of the house for a few!"

The friends had settled right back into their good-natured banter. It was almost like Jules was there with her. *Almost.*

India rolled over to glance at the clock, and then shot out of bed with a start.

"Oh my God, Jules . . . I have that welcome dinner in, like, thirty minutes, and I have total sleep-face. I have to go scotch-tape myself together. I'll call you tomorrow. Love you, bye!"

She barely heard her friend urge her to go before she rushed to the bathroom to see what she was working with.

Oh. OK.

The crazy-lunatic-meets-ragged-out-rock-star look wouldn't fly here. Her go-to messy braid was clearly in order.

She threw on a long suede skirt, riding boots, and a white belted off-the-shoulder peasant top she had packed for the welcome dinner. That left her three minutes to apply some mascara and a swipe of lip gloss. *Not bad,* she thought, minus the pillow crease on her cheek, but hopefully that would fade once she hit the fresh air.

She grabbed the key to the cottage, switched off the lights, and slipped out the door. Pausing for a moment, she decided that she had just enough time to walk to the pavilion rather than taking her golf cart. It was such a beautiful evening. It would be a shame to miss the chance to stroll along the gorgeous landscape.

He was barely out of the truck before his favorite three-year-old was stumbling down the porch steps of the farmhouse on her chubby little toddler legs, making a beeline for her uncle Wyatt.

"Hold you! *Up!* Mwah!"

Wyatt gladly accepted Sadie's moist little kisses on the side of his stubbly face. This was the best part about coming home. He felt so loved here, and he realized in that moment just how much he'd missed them.

He gave the little girl a big squeeze.

"Hi, toots! Do Mama and Daddy know you're out here?"

He carried her up the steps, and he was just about to rap on the screen door, when he saw Violet making her way toward him from the rear of the house.

"Mama! Uncle Wyatt is home," Sadie sang, her little milk teeth gleaming inside her broad smile.

Her mother was just as enthusiastic, pushing open the screen door and enveloping Wyatt in a warm embrace.

"Welcome home, stranger," she said.

Rex was right behind her, equally eager to greet his friend.

"Hey, man, long time no see. Now it's a party, huh, Sadie?"

The toddler reached for her daddy's arms, and Wyatt reluctantly let her scramble onto Rex like a baby monkey.

"How about a cold one? They're brewing up some pretty great stuff here these days."

Rex was fond of all the farm had to offer, but the craft beer was a particular favorite. Blackberry Farm had started brewing their own beer several years back, and they were earning quite a reputation within the industry.

"Sounds awesome. Thanks, man. It's great to see you guys."

Wyatt accepted the beer with a tap against Rex's own bottle.

"How the heck has little miss gotten so big? Is Finn sprinkling that organic fertilizer of his on her at night?"

Sadie puffed up at the mention and wiggled down to return to her coloring books, which were sprawled around the coffee table.

"Well, get in here and tell us what you've been up to since we FaceTimed you in Alaska."

Violet led them to the kitchen table, where she had set out cheese and crackers.

"Didn't you say you were finishing up your trip in Washington State?"

Violet was always captivated by the stories Wyatt brought home to them. She was the only other person he could talk to about his experiences behind the lens who understood him completely. Rex was a fine photographer in his own right, but his passion had shifted to video editing in recent years, so he didn't quite share the same perspective as his wife and best friend. They talked several times a week, but it had been a few days since they'd properly caught up. Violet plopped down in a chair, resting her chin in her hand, waiting for the details.

Wyatt kicked back in his chair, taking a long drag of his beer before answering her.

"Yeah, I was up in Snoqualmie, doing a piece on the falls. It's tough to do it justice, though, because there's a power plant at the top on one side, and a resort on the other, so I had to get creative with my angles. It's a beauty, though. The lighting is spectacular, and the green in those Northwest forests is just a different color. It's the constant rain and mist, I guess."

Wyatt reached for the cheese and crackers. He didn't realize how hungry he was.

"Hey, what are you guys doing for dinner tonight? Can I crash?"

He knew he was always welcome, and it was a sort of tradition for them to share his homecoming meal together when he returned to town. But they were usually at Rex and Violet's duplex in Knoxville. The farmhouse was just their temporary home base while Violet taught at Blackberry.

"Actually, I wanted to talk to you about that."

Violet smiled at Wyatt and angled herself so she was looking more directly at him.

"Uh, why do I suddenly feel nervous? That grin. What do you want? Do I have to cook? Are we having some new vegan creation? Rex, tell me she didn't make you sell the barbecue."

Wyatt was teasing her, but he knew something was up. He'd known her too long not to read her that way.

"No, no. Don't worry, you'll get your belly filled with Blackberry Farm deliciousness. Besides, I'm Paleo this week, so the barbecue stays. For now."

Wyatt laughed at the relieved look on Rex's face.

"We're hosting a welcome dinner out at the Yallerhammer tonight for our student guests," Violet continued. "We want you to join us. Susan already agreed to let Sadie spend the night with her, bless her soul."

Rex sprouted a predatory grin, prompting Violet to give his arm a gentle punch.

"He thinks that means I'll drink a bunch of wine so he can have his way with me. There's a pretty good chance of that, actually," she mused, and the three friends laughed together.

Wyatt took a swig of his beer and leaned back on two legs of his chair.

"Why don't you guys go to dinner alone? I don't want to crash your workshop thing. I can grab dinner over in the barn."

He was well aware that India would probably be attending the dinner, and he was sure that he'd crossed paths with her enough for one day. Although it was more than a little tempting to clap eyes on her again, he thought better of it. He had the sense that she could be a slippery slope for him.

"No way! You're coming. We insist," Violet said. "Besides, we already have a place set for you, so it would be rude to have them switch everything around at this point." Violet nodded, the issued settled in her mind. "There is just one more teeny-tiny thing."

She and Rex exchanged a knowing look before turning their collective gaze back to Wyatt. Violet took a deep breath.

"What are your plans for the next year?"

Wyatt had just drained the last of his beer. Fortunately, he'd had time to swallow before she'd spoken, or he would have given them both a hops shower.

"Why? What's going on? Did you win the lottery and you're taking me on a trip?"

He was only half kidding. It was their dream to travel together one day. See all of the places they hadn't yet, and take loads of photos of their dream locations.

The cliffside temples in Bhutan.

The ancient pyramids of Egypt.

For all he had done and seen with *National Geographic*, there was still so much left to do. Violet was smiling, so Wyatt knew it had to be something good.

"Not quite. I mean, Rex, Sadie, and I are going to be traveling around the word, but you're not exactly invited." She saw his shocked face register her words, and added, "Not this time anyway! But we need you. You can say no, but hear me out first."

Wyatt nodded his head and waited for her to continue. Violet stood up and started pacing anxiously around the kitchen while she spoke.

"I mean, we didn't see this coming. You know that piece we shot for *Town & Country* in the fall? The one where we talked about how Blackberry was on the cutting edge of a food revolution not only here in Tennessee but globally?"

Wyatt nodded. "Yeah, the one that made Finn strut around this place like a peacock for a month? I remember."

"Well, we were approached by a publisher to write a book about it, using our photographs and stories from people on the forefront of the movement all around the world. The catch is that we need the next year to travel and gather their stories. But we really want to do it, Wyatt. It's the opportunity of a lifetime for us."

Violet stopped pacing and squared up to hear his thoughts, her eyes sparkling and pleading with him.

He blew out a breath.

"Wow. That's incredible! I'm so happy for you guys. I've always said you were hiding your light under a bushel basket by staying local. I knew it was just a matter of time before you got your due. I'm confused, though. Why do you need me?"

Wyatt got up to throw his beer bottle into the recycle bin, then turned back toward them.

Rex chimed in. "She needs you to *be* her for the year, brother. She doesn't trust anyone else. We have all these photo workshops scheduled at the farm, and all of the marketing materials that need to be shot throughout the year. It's a full-time gig. So we were hoping you might agree to put down some roots for the next three hundred and sixty-five days or so."

Rex finished his beer, stood, and moved toward the sink where Wyatt was frozen in his tracks. Rex slapped him on the back.

"Don't worry. We're coming back. It's just a year. What do you say?"

The kitchen was silent except for the sound of the crickets and frogs starting to fire up outside the screen door. Wyatt looked between them, first at Rex, then to Violet. How could he say no to them? They'd been his rock, his foundation. As much as the thought of being in one place for a year terrified him, he heard himself agreeing before his brain could craft a reason not to.

Violet shrieked and bounced over to plant a big kiss on his cheek.

"Oh, Wyatt, you are just the best friend ever. I know it's going to be a big adjustment for you, but we think you'll settle right back in to a life here."

Violet saw him pale a bit at the thought.

"A temporary life! And you'll be surprised at how much creative license you can take within the confines of this gig. The timing is perfect. We want you to help teach the workshop that starts tomorrow so you can get a sense of how we structure the itineraries. It's settled. We'll introduce you at dinner tonight, so get yourself dressed. We have to be there in thirty minutes, so see if you can come up with something presentable to wear."

Violet gave him another quick peck on the cheek, and Rex slapped him on the shoulder. They rushed over and grabbed Sadie and hustled upstairs to get ready, leaving him standing there in the kitchen, wondering what the hell had just happened to his life.

CHAPTER
SIX

As India rounded the bend, having passed by the barn and a weathered-looking covered bridge, she was rewarded for choosing to walk that evening. Ahead in the distance, she could see the Yallerhammer Pavilion awash in candlelight, casting a stunning mirror image onto the still pond it was perched above. The sky was peppered with starlight, and she could smell the combination of wood smoke and the evening's culinary delights wafting toward her as she drew nearer.

It was a feast for her senses.

Under the roof of the pavilion, there was a bustle of activity, likely the staff making final preparations for the evening. She slowed her gait, taking time to listen to the sounds of the nighttime creatures and their forest symphony. Ahead, she saw the lights of a golf cart swing into place next to the pond's dock. Three people climbed out and headed toward the pavilion—from the looks of it, two men and a woman.

Off to her left, horses grazed in a large fenced pasture, but they were slowly being rounded up by ranch hands to head back to the barn for the evening. One of the horses whinnied softly as she passed.

India was glad she'd come. It felt like she never got this kind of alone time or connection with nature back in New York. Sure, she could zip out to the Hamptons, but convening with nature there meant standing barefoot on the trimmed grass on a billionaire's bocce ball court, next to a clapboard seaside mansion.

It didn't have quite the same effect.

Yes, she needed this time to reflect and figure some things out, and she planned to maximize every moment. She made a mental note to try to get up early enough the next morning to shoot the Yallerhammer at first light. She imagined it would be a whole different experience than the one she'd have this evening.

As she neared the final turnoff, she noticed that the pavilion's deck was now filled with guests, some holding rocks glasses, most in groups of two or three, chatting. She climbed the steps leading into the space and graciously accepted the offer of a signature gin cocktail from one of the servers.

It was an eclectic crowd; there were people of all ages, from a couple in their early thirties to an elderly group of ladies, and everything in between. As the crowd ebbed, she spotted a twosome that she assumed must be the hosts, by the way they were animatedly talking with a group of captivated guests.

The woman was gorgeous; she was as tall as India but different in every other way. Her red hair was long and thick, framing her porcelain features exquisitely. Her green eyes sparkled as she looked at her husband, who was great-looking in his own right. He stood several inches taller than his wife, his handsome face and goatee reminding India of a famous country singer she'd interviewed a few weeks prior.

She slipped through the masses, making her way toward the duo. As she got closer, she could hear the woman suggest that they get the evening under way, and India watched as she nudged her husband toward the back of the deck to begin their welcome remarks.

With a gentle tap of fork against glass, Violet got the attention of the crowd and began the evening's festivities.

"Welcome, everyone! I'm Violet, and this is my handsome and supremely talented partner and husband, Rex. Thank you for joining us tonight at the very beautiful Yallerhammer Pavilion to kick off our Behind the Lens event. We're thrilled to have you share this special evening with us. I recognize a few old friends of the farm, and I'm pleased to see several new faces too. It's going to be a wonderful week. A toast to you all for making this journey!"

Violet raised her glass, and the night air was filled with the sounds of crystal meeting crystal. Violet took a quick sip of her drink, letting the murmurs die down.

"Tomorrow we'll get down to the brass tacks, but tonight is about making friends with your fellow workshoppers. We've taken the liberty of placing name cards at each setting, hoping to mix and mingle you in the most perfect and unexpected way. But before we begin, just a couple of announcements.

"First, we'll be meeting tomorrow in the teaching kitchen up at the barn. Our award-winning chef, Roger Mend, has arranged for us to watch a cooking demonstration, so that we might practice some still-life or commercial photography while we learn his tricks of the trade. I like to start this way for two reasons: One, it's a great way to keep us all in close-enough proximity so, if we have questions, they are easily answered for the benefit of the group. And two, there's rain in the forecast tomorrow, so let's try to stay dry on day one, shall we?"

The crowd laughed, nodding their heads in agreement.

"One last thing. My husband, Rex, and I are thrilled to welcome a surprise guest instructor for the week. We've personally known him since he was a very young man; heck, I guess we were all pretty young back then."

Another murmur of laughter.

"He's an award-winning photographer for *National Geographic*, and he's sure to offer you a most unique perspective, especially once we move out into the woods and begin the landscape portion of the week. He also happens to be one of my favorite people on the planet. Please give a warm welcome to our good friend, and a very talented guy, Mr. Wyatt Hinch."

Wyatt had been hanging back against the rail, under the shadow of the eaves, watching the crowd with growing interest.

That's not true.

He'd been watching India.

Wyatt saw her shyly enter the party and accept her drink. He watched her assess the crowd, as if she were collecting data to process later, and then zero in quickly on Violet and Rex.

He watched her face go from a pleasant smile to realization to outright shock at the announcement of his name.

He felt a thrill when he registered another emotion in her eyes. Excitement.

It had flickered across her face before she could help it or notice him, and it was in that moment that he knew he had to kiss her. It would be on her terms, but it was inevitable as far as he was concerned. He was bewitched.

Wyatt pushed himself off the rail and ambled over to where Violet and Rex were waiting. He nodded his thanks and then murmured something about not being much for public speaking, but India didn't even try to make out what he was saying.

Because the whole time, he was staring right at her like she was going to be his dinner. There was no fighting the blush this time; she could only hope that the candlelight would dim the effect. It probably hadn't, though, because the minute she felt it bloom across her face, Wyatt gave her an almost imperceptible smile and then turned the remarks back over to his friends.

Water. Water would be a great idea right now. Where are the waiters with water?

She was thinking in alliterations now.

Damn it.

OK, find a reason to move around, she thought. *Find the table with your name card,* she decided. India folded back into the crowd and made her way to the table that held the seating placards. She spent a moment finding hers, then turned around to head to her table. She stopped short at the sight of him, just there, in front of her.

"We meet again," Wyatt said with a wry smile.

India felt an involuntary shudder sweep across her bare shoulders, despite the warm evening air. He looked like he had just stepped out of the pages of the *GQ* Rugged Man edition. Upon closer inspection, his wavy hair had the tiniest dusting of pepper and the curls had been tamed with something that smelled out of this world. Since she last saw him in the garden, he'd changed into a plaid shirt, worn under a weathered-looking jacket, and an unbelievable pair of jeans.

Oh, the jeans.

Other men should stop wearing them. They could never compete.

The stubble along his jawline moved as he smiled at her, flashing that single dimple and watching with obvious satisfaction as she gave him the same once-over that he'd given her a few moments earlier.

He snapped her back to attention with that voice.

"India, I want to assure you, this opportunity came as a complete surprise to me. I never intended to become your new best friend this week. Violet and Rex approached me just this afternoon with the idea of teaching with them, and although I realized right away that it might be a little weird for you, I couldn't say no to them. They're the two people in this world who have always been there for me. So this is about that, not about me stalking you."

He paused, lowering his chin to aim his gaze more directly into her eyes and said, "Although I'm not going to pretend I'm disappointed to have the opportunity to spend a little more time with you."

He took a step closer and then reached around her, inadvertently brushing his arm against hers as he searched for his place card from the table. The scent of him was heady stuff, and she skittered back a few feet to provide him a wider berth, and to try to get her goose bumps to disappear before he noticed them. He was catnip, and she was acting like a depraved alley cat. She had to regroup here.

"Oh, it's fine, I didn't think anything of it," she assured him with a dismissive wave of her hand.

When he appeared to question her denial with a crooked eyebrow, she quickly added, "I mean, I was surprised to hear about your photography credentials, considering we discussed the workshop this morning and you didn't mention them, but I guess maybe you didn't feel like getting too deep with a stranger. It's cool. I look forward to learning from you, though; it sounds like you've got the chops to make this one heck of a workshop. I'm sure I'll learn a lot."

He looked surprised at her rebuff. India knew exactly the effect she was having.

She finished him off with a chilly, "Hey, have a fun time tonight. And great speech, by the way," patting the top of his arm in a sisterly gesture to add insult to injury.

With that, she whirled around, and zigzagged her way between the tables until she found her assigned seat. India was relieved to find herself flanked by a buxom woman who looked to be in her late forties and a burly man with a long white beard. Wyatt, who she noticed out of the corner of her eye was still smarting from her blow-off, had sulked his way to an adjoining table, situating himself in his spot across from Violet and next to Rex.

India sat down, adjusted her napkin, and proceeded to have great conversations with her tablemates. Jeff, the bearded gentleman, was from Austin, and he was already a fairly accomplished photographer, as the owner of a full time in a vintage camera shop in the artsy Texas town. They chatted about their respective equipment, and he promised to take a look at what India had collected for herself over the years and make some recommendations to her during class tomorrow. While she found their conversation stimulating, she couldn't help stealing occasional glances at Wyatt.

Every time she looked, he seemed to be engrossed in serious conversation with his friends. She felt a small seed of panic rise up. She hadn't meant to be such a bitch, but she'd had to do something to change the momentum. She didn't want him to get the wrong idea; she was here to work on herself, not play games. She'd gotten good over the years at deflecting, and after her latest epic romantic fiasco, she'd fallen right back in to her old pattern of dodge and run. This was ground she knew how to cover.

India sighed and gamely turned her attention to her other dining companion, the well-heeled redhead on her left. Annabelle had left her husband at home in Atlanta this trip, bringing her daughter, Virginia, instead. Both women sported colossal diamonds on their ring fingers, but they didn't appear to spend much of their free time thinking about their better halves. Instead, they had fixated on Wyatt, making it difficult for India to continue her attempted strategy of completely ignoring him.

"I swear, that man is absolutely darling. How lucky are we to get to spend the week with such a specimen?"

It was a little difficult to understand Annabelle; maybe it was the accent, or perhaps it was because her voluptuous mouth was pinched into a manmade trout pout. Virginia understood her mother perfectly, however, and nodded in robust agreement.

"He is delicious," she purred in fluent Georgia peach. "Don't think I won't maneuver my way into his . . . class . . . this week." She winked at her mother, and they both chortled.

India's appetite vanished in an instant.

Poor Wyatt. He was going to be eaten alive by these predators. She instinctively glanced back over at him, and this time, he was focused right on her. They locked gazes as he picked up his wineglass, and then he continued his conversation without missing a beat.

"I don't know what's made you so irritable, Wyatt," Violet said, clearly surprised by his behavior so far during dinner. "I mean, you shouldn't have said yes if you meant no," she whispered with an exasperated sigh. "And what do you keep scowling at?" Violet followed his gaze over her shoulder to the graceful-looking blonde woman with rosy cheeks who was sitting at the next table. The woman caught Violet's glance and hurriedly busied herself with cutlery, her blush deepening.

Violet swung back around and looked at Wyatt.

"Wyatt, do you know that woman?"

Then it dawned on her. He did know her, somehow. And, astonishingly, Violet knew her too. She watched India every morning while she fixed Sadie's breakfast. She studied Wyatt's face for any sign that he knew who India really was but decided that he was oblivious.

Wasn't that interesting?

He'd definitely get spooked if he found out she'd just called off the wedding of the year. Better to keep that morsel to herself for now. This was the kind of woman Wyatt needed: strong, independent. And it didn't look like chemistry would be a problem.

Violet knew raw attraction when she saw it, and she'd seen Wyatt like this before. Problem was, he always morphed into asshole Wyatt almost immediately, so any woman who looked his way would get turned off and leave him alone. Not this time. Not so fast.

Wyatt watched the realization play across Violet's face, and panicked. Damn. She knew. Now he was in deep trouble. Rex nudged Wyatt in the shoulder and shook his head.

"Brother, you should know better than to show your hand like that. Have I taught you nothing?"

Violet kicked Rex under the table, smiling sweetly when he reached down to rub his shin. She'd show these two knuckleheads. Violet had waited a long time for this opportunity, and here it had simply fallen into her lap like a gift.

"I just met her briefly this morning, and I'm not scowling at her. I don't know enough about her to scowl. I'm just . . . I'm just adjusting to the idea that my whole life is about to change. I said I'd stay, and I will. Just give me some time to make the adjustment. Now quit chirping at me and eat your dessert." Wyatt knew he was rambling, the same way he knew Violet could see through him like no one else. It was over.

She would have her bow and arrow dusted off, ready to play Cupid before the week was over.

And the way he was staring at India?

Violet smiled.

It would be like shooting fish in a barrel.

CHAPTER
SEVEN

After dinner, the festivities shifted out to a spot near the pond, where the staff had staged a roaring bonfire, complete with wooden rocking chairs and flickering tin lanterns. The woolen blankets draping the chairs were a nice touch, but the evening was still warm enough, so most guests didn't use them. A bluegrass band was set up using the woods as a backdrop, and the pleasing sounds of the fiddle added a welcome gaiety to the event.

There was a rustic wooden table set near the fire, with all the fixings for s'mores sprawled out across it. India circled around the back side, making a play for the beverage end of the table instead. Coffee with Baileys would be just the thing to ease her jangled nerves.

It had been more of the same from the mother-daughter team, who had all but mentally undressed and had their way with Wyatt during dessert. India tried very hard not to slap some sense into one or both of them, since they were making it impossible for her to think about anything but Wyatt. She hadn't looked back at him for the rest of the meal, but she could feel his burning gaze lighting up her traitorous cheeks even without visual confirmation.

India grasped her coffee and was already looking forward to an early exit so she could enjoy the stroll back to the cottage, when she saw Violet approaching her with a friendly smile.

"I've been trying to get around to everyone to say hello, but we seem to keep missing each other."

Violet placed a gentle hand on India's arm and gestured toward the steaming cup in her hand.

"I see we're gonna get along just fine, though." She grinned, reaching for her own cup. "This stuff is the best part about dinner at the Yallerhammer. Well, that and the cute mandolin player in the band." She winked.

India looked over and noticed that Rex was sitting in on this song, "The Lighthouse's Tale," which was one of her favorites.

"He grew up in a musical family. I swear he can play about ten different instruments. He's definitely handy at parties," she finished with a smile.

India could see why Wyatt loved Violet; she was as friendly and kind as she was beautiful. She looked like something out of those magazines back on India's coffee table at home, with her flowing hair and perfect skin, which had only been kissed with a hint of makeup. She stood eye to eye with India, which was rare, even with India wearing her flat riding boots.

An outsider might think that these two women shouldn't be allowed to stand together; it unfairly stacked the deck for the rest of the ladies at the gathering. All of that imposing beauty in one place. Violet gestured for India to follow her to a couple of rockers sitting at the outskirts of the fire.

"So what brings you to Blackberry Farm?" Violet asked. "Well, besides this spectacular photography workshop!"

India laughed softly, fiddling with the top of her cup. As she began to speak, it occurred to her that she'd better be careful about how much she shared. She valued the anonymity she knew she could enjoy here if she played it close to the vest.

"I was supposed to be spending the week with my best friend, but her daughter got sick at the last minute, so it's just me."

India shrugged her shoulders.

"It's OK, though. I don't get a lot of alone time where I live, and my job is pretty demanding, so I figured I should take advantage of this opportunity."

She turned toward Violet.

"Your workshop is the best part, though. I've always been interested in being on this side of the camera," she said.

India paused, catching the slip, and looked up to see if Violet had noticed. It was obvious she had.

"Don't worry. Your secret is safe with me," Violet assured her. "No one here has to know who you are unless you decide to tell them." She leaned in to India, lowering her voice before adding, "But I mean, come on. I have a three-year-old, and we play Barbies while we watch you almost every morning. There aren't many mommies who wouldn't recognize you in an instant. Lucky for you, most of the guests here are either retired or young couples that work hard and play hard. They don't have time for morning television. You should be able to fly under the radar, for once."

She paused and, seeing India's obvious relief, added, "I hope that brings you some peace."

India sighed deeply, relieved because Violet knew who she was but clearly wasn't going to bring up the whole wedding fiasco. India thanked her, and the women sat together in comfortable silence for a few moments.

"So, about Wyatt," Violet started.

India's head snapped up.

Violet grinned. "Funny, he had the same reaction when I asked about you at dinner. Don't worry. If my radar is any good, he doesn't have a clue about your job, or anything else about you." Violet gazed out over the fire, then back to India. "If you don't mind me asking, though, how did you two meet?"

Violet took a sip of the steaming coffee, waiting for India to fill in the blanks.

India was thoughtful for a moment. "I was caught off guard at the airport this morning when I found out that Julia—my friend—wasn't going to make it. In a moment of weakness, I got a little weepy—classic public meltdown. Anyway, Wyatt happened to be nearby and offered his help. Long story short, he heard I was headed here, so he offered me a ride. That's it. That's really the whole story."

She turned to scan the other guests, instinctively looking for Wyatt, and found him sitting on top of a picnic table holding a rocks glass filled with something. He was talking to Rex, who had finished up his set with the band and had rejoined his friend. As if Wyatt somehow felt her sizing them up, he turned and met her gaze from across the fire pit. He didn't look away, instead mumbling something to Rex, who chuckled and punched him in the shoulder good-naturedly. Wyatt rewarded India with that grin once more and then turned his attention back to Rex.

India hated herself for getting caught staring at him again. Feeling predictable, she bristled silently.

"You know, something did bother me about Wyatt. I mentioned to him earlier that I was attending your workshop this weekend, and while he sang your praises as a teacher, he failed to mention his own credentials. I find that strange." It still puzzled and irritated her that he hadn't been forthcoming when he'd had the chance.

Violet turned toward India and began to speak with great fondness about her friend. "Wyatt is an amazingly talented man, but he's been alone for a long time, so his social skills can be a little rusty."

It was obvious Violet cared about him.

"Don't hold it against him. I'm sure if you'd had more time together, he would have shared that piece of his story with you. Believe me. I've known him a long time, and he is one of the kindest, most honest, most genuine people I know. He's not the kind of man who plays games. I honestly don't think he would know how. He's suffered a lot for someone so young."

Violet paused, considering her next words carefully.

"But that's his story to tell. I will say, I truly believe he's finally ready to try to figure out what's next for him, but he's not sure where to begin."

India felt bad about being harsh with him earlier. It made sense to her now. She wondered how a man like Wyatt had managed to remain alone for so long, and why. She looked back at Violet. "I understand. Plan B can be a real bitch."

They nodded in silent agreement, sipping their coffees, as the logs crackled in the dying fire.

"If you want to go talk to her, why don't you move your ass and tell my wife to beat it?" Rex slapped Wyatt on the shoulder and nudged him over to make room for himself at the picnic table. He handed Wyatt a glass. "Single malt, old enough to get the job done." He snickered. Wyatt clinked glasses with Rex in a wordless toast.

Rex let out a whistle. "Seriously, I'm surprised you're letting Vi have all that unsupervised face time with her. Who knows what she's saying about you." Rex sported a Cheshire grin as Wyatt squirmed uncomfortably at the thought.

Wyatt returned his attention to the women and found India once again looking directly back at him.

"Damn," he muttered to Rex. "I think I might be in over my head with her. It's been a long time, bro. Obviously too long."

Rex elbowed his friend, and they broke into comfortable laughter. Wyatt smiled at her again, in spite of himself, before turning away to try to preserve a shred of his dignity.

Rex paused and then said what they were both thinking. "Maybe it's finally time, Wyatt. Do you think you could get out of your own way for once?"

The musicians wrapped up their final song, and the few guests that were left around the bonfire stood to call it a night.

Wyatt decided it was now or never. Rex was right. Wyatt knew she'd walked to the pavilion from her cottage; he'd been waiting and watching for her when she'd arrived.

He stood up and motioned for Rex to follow him. He let out a breath and then headed over to where Violet and India were saying their good-byes. As they approached, both women turned their way, Violet smiling, and India watching them curiously.

"Wyatt, India tells me you've met." Smiling innocently, Violet linked hands with her husband and continued, "Would you mind terribly walking her back to Woodshed? Rex and I would give her a ride, but we need to stay and wrap things up with the band. I'd hate to make her wait, and you know this place so well."

Violet waited expectantly. The energy being exchanged between Wyatt and India was palpable.

Wyatt hadn't been prepared for Violet to beat him to the punch. India looked equally surprised, but she recovered first.

"Oh gosh, it's OK. Wyatt's already had to drive me around once today. I had a lovely walk down here, so I'm sure I'll be just fine on the way back." India smiled at Wyatt, and he could tell she was trying to let him off the hook.

Wyatt cleared his throat. Plan B.

"I'd actually like to walk you back, if it's OK with you." The air seemed to form a vacuum as they awaited her response.

CHAPTER
EIGHT

Wyatt and India said their good-byes to Violet and Rex and then headed down the moonlit path leading away from the pond. The evening was alive now with the sounds of unseen woodland creatures, lending an eerie vibe India hadn't noticed earlier. Maybe it was the stillness of the inky night that was unsettling, or perhaps it was the closeness of this man who had some inexplicable effect on her. She had to figure out a way to slow her pulse, reminding herself to keep her breath as steady as possible as they set out on the path in silence. The evening wasn't cool, so there was no explanation for the goose bumps that traveled across her neck and shoulders. She let out an involuntary shiver.

Wyatt could tell she was skittish. Hell, he was nervous himself. He really had no idea what he was doing. He was drawn to her in a way that he hadn't experienced with any woman since—well, in a very long time. He noticed her shiver, and wondered how she could be cold when he was so damned hot.

Shrugging out of his jacket, he slowed his step.

"Here, take my coat. It's cooler now that we're away from the fire, and we have a ways to go."

She paused and didn't protest when he draped the garment around her bare shoulders, thanking him with a smile.

Those bare shoulders. He'd wondered what her skin felt like there. Was it as soft and warm as it looked? He'd had a hard time all night concentrating on anything else, really. He'd caught the scent of her as he leaned close to drape the coat around her, and he immediately felt betrayed by his own body. He flushed and cleared his throat, hoping he could reclaim some control.

He wanted her. Badly.

India's senses were overwhelmed. Wrapping herself in his jacket was almost like being in his arms. The smell of him was intoxicating, and she struggled to thank him for the gesture. She supposed she owed him an apology for her abrupt dismissal earlier that evening.

"I'm really sorry I was so crisp before. I didn't mean to be dismissive. I guess I was just surprised that you didn't mention your job when we were talking about photography earlier. Honestly, I overslept before dinner, and I think I might have been a little grumpy after waking up so late."

She pulled his jacket closer around her as they passed by the old barn.

Wyatt conjured up the image of India sleeping in that big bed in Woodshed he'd stayed in himself many times, and he shifted uncomfortably as he lost the battle with his body. He'd thought she looked sleepy when she'd arrived. Sleepy in a just-rolled-out-of-bed kind of way. He worked hard to focus on the path before them.

"I probably should have said something, but I didn't want to sound like some know-it-all," he said. "Besides, everything I've been able to do in my career is because of Violet, and you were on your way to her workshop, not mine."

India raised her eyebrows at that.

"Turns out, I'm going to be studying under you now anyway," she said.

The thought of her studying anything under him was too much to bear. He steered the conversation back to safety.

"That is a new development. Rex and Violet have an opportunity to travel for a while, so I'm going to take over here while they're away. They want to show me the ropes this week. And so, I'm teaching."

He turned to her and slowed his pace.

"I promise you, I wasn't trying to be vague. And I'm really glad we'll get to work together. This really is the most incredible place to discover through the lens. It's amazing for me to see it through the eyes of a first-time guest."

India felt herself starting to relax a little. It was easy to talk with him, and he was clearly invigorated by photography.

"Your job sounds amazing. What's it like to travel for a living? It must get lonely, being away from your family and friends so much."

Wyatt tucked his hands into the top of his jeans pockets as they resumed their pace.

"Honestly, I love my job. I've traveled all around and seen some incredible places. It's a dream job for a photographer, for sure. I will say, in the last couple of years, I've noticed that it's gotten more difficult to leave and more rewarding to come home. Violet and Rex have the most amazing little girl now, and I hate the fact that I'm missing out on seeing her grow up."

The little girl in the photo on his dashboard. India smiled, listening to Wyatt talk about Violet and her family in the same way Violet had spoken so fondly of him.

"I can tell how close the three of you are—you, Violet, and Rex, I mean. They seem like lovely people. You've known them a long time?"

She was aware that the journalist in her was digging for information, but she couldn't help herself. She wanted to know his story.

"They saved me from myself, really."

He paused, changing course.

"Violet showed me that photography could be healing, and she got me an interview at *National Geographic* at a critical time for me personally. The job gave me my life back. I guess that's what makes me question whether or not I can survive in one place. I've been a rolling stone for so long."

"I guess you're about to find out." India smiled.

He'd been through something serious; that much was clear. It made her want to open up a little in return.

"My job has been my life too. I love it, I do."

Their eyes met, and his expression encouraged her to continue.

"I've wondered lately if there isn't something missing, though. In fact, I was this close to getting married in December, but at the last minute, I knew it wasn't right."

She looked at him intently now as they had both slowed back down. She sighed.

"So. Plan B."

He nodded in silent agreement.

Wyatt couldn't figure how someone could have let her go. In all honesty, he was relieved to hear that she wasn't interested in marriage. He couldn't imagine himself as a husband again. But that didn't make him desire her any less. In fact, her vulnerability made her even sexier.

And his greatest relief was hearing that she was single.

They walked in silence for a few more minutes, each lost in their own thoughts. They rounded the bend, and Woodshed came into view. It looked so cozy, with the windows spilling out soft light and a plume of smoke rising up from the chimney. India could smell the fire, grateful for the staff that had prepared her cottage for the evening.

"Isn't it a cool place?" Wyatt asked. "It's my favorite of all of the accommodations on the property. I like being so near the fields too. I'm close with Finn, our master gardener. That's who I was talking with today. Make sure you take a walk over to his planting shed. Just allow enough time; he's passionate about what he does, and he'll talk your ear off if you get him started about heirloom seeds."

India smiled.

"I've actually read about him in *Food and Wine* magazine. There's a guy who loves what he does. I'm definitely planning a visit with him."

They'd arrived at her cottage and were now standing on the path looking out over the fields, which were bathed in moonlight. There was the shiver again, reminding India that she should return his jacket. She turned sideways to offer it back to him.

"Thank you once again for your chivalry. Your jacket kept me warm, but it sure looked better on you."

Did she really just say that?

Wyatt stepped closer, gently lifting the coat off her, dipping his head to catch her scent once more. A heat rose off her, and before he knew what he was doing, he let his fingertips lightly graze her bare shoulder.

Soft, yes. Like fine silk. And so warm. He stiffened when she shivered in an instant reply.

India closed her eyes at his touch.

She turned back toward him, their faces just inches apart. His eyes searched hers for what to do next, but before he could read her, she had taken a step toward him and had risen up to place the softest kiss on his jawline. She backed away quickly, licking her bottom lip nervously.

"Thank you, Wyatt."

She was sure he could hear her heartbeat; it was over-whelmingly loud in her own ears. She summoned up the courage to take it further.

"Would you like to stay and have a drink with me on the porch?"

His emotions were clashing inside him. He'd never been this aroused, of that he was sure. But he felt guilty, as if he were betraying a memory. Even so, he craved that taste of her that he had allowed himself to fantasize about earlier. But he decided to use the last of his wits to stop himself from taking this too far.

"Thanks, but we both have a full day tomorrow. I'll see you in the morning at the barn. Eleven, right?"

He thought he saw a flicker of surprise and disappoint-ment in her eyes as he turned to walk back down the porch steps.

"Sure, of course. See you at eleven."

India was both relieved and horrified. What had she hoped to accomplish by offering him a drink? No wonder he'd practically run out of there. She had just opened the door to go inside when she heard his voice.

"What the hell."

Wyatt had turned around, and he was bounding back up the path toward her. He took the door and kept it propped open against his back. She stood frozen on the threshold, staring up at him with those blue eyes. She was illuminated from behind by the fire, making her appear to him like an angel. He took her face in his hands, staring intently back at her as if searching for something, then slowly lowered his lips to meet hers.

The first graze was soft, almost imperceptible. She felt breathless as his stubble grazed her slightly parted lips. She inhaled sharply. His second pass hit the bull's-eye. She opened her mouth a little more, inviting him in to explore.

They couldn't get enough of each other.

She tasted of coffee and cream liquor; Wyatt of Scotch and wood smoke. His hands left her face, traveled along her neck, pausing to play gently with the hair at her nape, and finally skimmed to a stop on the back of her shoulders.

She instinctively reached up to him, allowing him to explore her mouth more deeply, feeling his desire for her.

Wyatt was vaguely aware that he was losing control.

He could never get enough of her; he knew that now.

He reluctantly broke their kiss and leaned back, turning to go.

"Good night," he told her, smiling gently as his hands slid off her shoulders and down her arms. He stepped backward, and before India could speak, Wyatt was headed down the path and had disappeared into the evening.

CHAPTER
NINE

Wyatt cranked up the music on his iPod as loud as it would go and finally felt himself break a sweat. Eminem informed him that he only had one shot, and that this opportunity comes once in a lifetime. He tried not to think about how that seemed to directly apply to him lately.

Mornings on the farm were special. Wyatt loved to get up before the sun, strap on his running shoes, and head out before most guests had had their first cup of coffee. This morning, the air was cool, and a silvery mist rose up off the warm waters of Walland pond, making the boathouse look like a painting. There was no breeze, so the only movement was the wake in the water being left by a pair of mallards who'd risen earlier than he had.

His feet thumped against the pavement in sync with the music as he felt the adrenaline start to kick in. His plan was to run the perimeter of the fields and then stop by the garden to help Finn stage the heavy bags of soil before hitting the shower and heading to the barn. His mind wandered as he rounded the bend and ran past the small family cemetery on the hill. It was usually a place he stopped for a few moments, but today he picked up his pace and sped by.

What had he done? He thought he'd been smart, dragging himself off that porch before she noticed how desperate he was to touch her. But that palpable vulnerability of hers. He couldn't leave her standing there thinking that she was undesirable; he could see her confusion when he'd declined the drink. He'd only been trying to be a gentleman, but trying wasn't succeeding.

He'd obviously lost all reason when he turned around to go back to her. Now, he wondered if he'd taken too much.

That kiss was ridiculous.

It had taken every fiber of his being to finally pull away. He'd left before she could say anything, and all night he'd lain awake, those eyes of hers haunting him as he tried to figure out the thoughts behind them. He hoped she wouldn't be uncomfortable around him in class today. He resolved to be strictly professional so she wouldn't have any reason to be uneasy. His new resolve helped him accelerate up the last big hill and into the garden, where Finn stood waiting for him in the early-morning light.

India was up early too, snuggled into the overstuffed sofa, her steaming cup of coffee starting to unscramble her brain. She was exhausted, but she couldn't spend another moment in that bed where she had fitfully tossed all night, reliving the previous evening.

She vacillated between cringing at her own pluck for inviting Wyatt to stay and the flutter she felt when she remembered the feel of his mouth on hers. She couldn't remember exactly, but she was pretty sure she had stopped breathing for a time.

She'd felt like a drunk who couldn't get enough to feel satisfied. It was as if her guts had been scooped out when he'd pulled away, and she'd spent way too long leaning against her closed door with her hand against her cheek, touching the place his stubble had rubbed her cheek raw.

She got up and walked into the bathroom to see if she was still pink from his touch. The woman staring back at her had changed. She couldn't figure out why, but she felt like she was looking at a stranger. She'd just shrugged out of her oversized T-shirt, preparing for a hot shower, when she remembered that she'd left the coffeepot on. She wrapped herself in one of the plush white towels and tiptoed out into the kitchen to turn it off. When she glanced out the window, the coffeepot was forgotten.

Finn was standing at the end of one of the rows of the garden with a wagon full of seedlings to plant. But that wasn't what had caught her attention.

Wyatt was striding toward him with a huge bag of soil slung over one shoulder. He'd been at it for a while, if his mud-and-sweat-caked back were any indication. He was wearing a baseball cap backward, his thick curls spilling out the bottom. He wore a pair of running shorts and sneakers, but not much else. His entire body glistened in the sun, beads of sweat and soil somehow enhancing his good looks. India started chewing on her finger absentmindedly. Her desire was tangible. She allowed herself a few more minutes of this riveting spectacle before finally tearing herself away from the window.

Forget the shower, she thought. She was going to want a few moments alone in that soaking tub. She hoped she could get herself together before class.

Mornings at Blackberry officially began with breakfast in the main house, so India jumped into her golf cart, figuring she'd have plenty of time to grab something to eat and take a short walk before heading back to the barn for class. She'd been hoping for one more peek at the action in the garden, but the rows were empty now, save for bags of soil at each row's end, ready to be spread.

India had just finished her breakfast and was enjoying her coffee in a cozy booth near the window when she spotted Violet and Rex, with Wyatt bringing up the rear, carrying their little girl. A hostess led them past her table toward another dining room. Violet, chatting with Rex, hadn't noticed India, but Wyatt was staring right at her.

"Morning," he said with a smile. She smiled back, answering him in kind, but was surprised when he kept on walking without stopping to talk. The little girl had been trying to braid the ends of his hair, she'd noticed. She saw the four of them sit down in the rear of the restaurant by the fireplace, Wyatt holding the child on his lap.

Her mind was racing now. Maybe he regretted the kiss? Violet had been the one to suggest he walk her home. What was the poor guy supposed to do, say no? Or maybe it hadn't had the same effect on him. She shook her head. Impossible. That kiss was epic. His body hadn't lied.

She finished her coffee and then scooted out of the dining room before they did, hoping to avoid a second humiliation. Stopping by the concierge desk, she grabbed a map of the hiking trails on the property and purchased some more bubble bath for her tub. Time to regroup. She'd head out that afternoon after class and lose herself in the woods, after which she'd enjoy a long hot bath with a good book and a giant glass of wine. That's why she'd come. To relax. Not to get all hot and bothered.

Wyatt was glad Violet had been distracted. He'd spotted India the moment they'd walked in. Damn, she was a knockout. Today, her hair was pulled back in a ponytail, and she was wearing a white button-down shirt with jeans and boots.

Effortless.

Even without much makeup, her face was luminous. He worked hard to avert his eyes.

Scooping Sadie up into his arms, Wyatt chuckled when she started pulling on his hair. She could be his excuse. He wanted to be professional with India to put her at ease. He smiled and said hello as they walked past, and she smiled back. *Better to keep the small talk to a minimum,* he thought, and he followed Rex and Vi to their table without stopping.

He positioned himself with his back to her so she wouldn't feel uncomfortable, but he couldn't help glancing over his shoulder to look for her a few moments later, only to see her table empty.

"Let me guess," Violet said, getting Wyatt's attention. "A certain someone just walked in." She grinned. "Why don't you go say good morning?" she asked.

Wyatt casually took a sip of his coffee while looking at the menu.

"She already left. And I did say good morning. I'm actually surprised at your rudeness; you two walked right by her."

Wyatt smirked as Violet looked horrified.

"Well, why didn't you say something? Jesus, Wyatt. I swear if I didn't know better I'd think you were raised by wolves." Violet sighed, reaching for the sugar and plopping three cubes into her mug. "So what happened last night? Did you find out her story?"

Violet watched for his reaction, but he denied her. He could play poker with the best of them.

Wyatt grabbed the bread basket and took a steaming biscuit into one hand, the butter dish in the other. He knew she was hoping for juicy details, but he wasn't ready to share just yet. Besides, he didn't know where they stood, and he didn't want to embarrass India—or himself. Violet could hold her horses.

"I walked her home, like you asked. No big deal. Although, next time, I can make the offer myself, thanks." He slathered butter onto the warm biscuit and then stuffed it into his mouth, indicating he was done discussing it.

Rex cracked up. "Man, I'm so glad to have someone else to share the heat. I'm usually the one in the crosshairs when you're gone, Wyatt. I gotta say, I think a year traveling together with my lovely bride is going to hurt me more than it's gonna hurt you."

Rex steeled his shin for a swift kick, but Violet only smiled sarcastically at the pair of them.

"Pardon me for wanting our best friend to have a life. You know, you could do worse, Wyatt. If you'd taken the time to get to know India at all, you'd be surprised at how smart and kind she is. That's part of her broad appeal."

The men looked at her with puzzled expressions.

"What do you mean 'broad appeal'?" Wyatt said. "She's not some movie star, is she? What am I missing here? How the hell could you know so much about her when you talked to her for the first time last night?"

Wyatt waited for Violet to answer.

"No, she's not a movie star, dummy. I just meant that even I could see how great she was after talking with her for a little while. I'm not asking you to propose, Wyatt. But would it kill you to ask her to dinner one of these nights, or show her a little attention when you breeze by her at breakfast? What, are you afraid to get to first base with a girl these days?" Violet joked with a sigh.

Wyatt had heard enough. He stood and flipped his napkin into the chair, sending Sadie scurrying into her mama's arms.

"For your information, first base wasn't a problem. And as far as India goes, I don't need anyone's encouragement to go there again. Thanks for your concern, though. Now let's go. Don't we have a class to teach?"

He turned and strode out of the restaurant, leaving Violet slack-jawed and Rex doubled over with laughter.

"I guess he told you, Vi," Rex said, chuckling.

He leaned over and went to first base with his own gorgeous but speechless wife.

CHAPTER
TEN

The barn was the crown jewel of Blackberry Farm. It was the first thing you saw driving in, all red reclaimed wood and pitched roofs, with large glass windows at the welcoming entrance. The inside housed the two-time James Beard Award–winning restaurant kitchens, along with a secondary teaching kitchen used by the frequent guest chefs and speakers.

On the lower level was a 160-thousand-bottle wine cellar that surrounded another space used for private dinners. The main dining room had a small area where musicians could entertain in an intimate setting, if they chose not to use the newer event center that had just been completed across the way.

Today, the barn's head chef would be preparing lunch for the group, allowing the students to photograph him at work, a special experience for everyone.

India stopped to watch the activity in the main kitchen for a few minutes on her way in. Chefs in white uniforms were already busy crafting the menus and completing food prep for that evening's dinner service. Even for India, who had dined at her fair share of amazing restaurants in Manhattan, this kitchen was impressive—not only in size but in cleanliness and efficiency too. Some of the best meals in the South were prepared by these hands. It was a privilege to observe, if only for a few moments before class.

India made her way over to where the group was assembling for the workshop. There were five rows of director's chairs facing the teaching kitchen, so she chose a chair near the end of the third row, in case she had to slip out to use the restroom.

Violet was up front, talking to a group of students, but she noticed India walk in and waved hello. Rex had set up a laptop at a table in the back, and he was huddled with Jeff, the photo-shop owner from Austin. India glanced around, aware she was looking for Wyatt, but she didn't see him. She climbed up into her director's chair and started glancing through the handout that had been left on the seat.

"How'd you sleep?"

His voice was low, but there was no mistaking it. She knew it was Wyatt without looking. Her body responded instantly, sending a tingle down her thighs. He'd walked up from behind her, but he was now heading down the row so he could face her. He rested his boot on the footrest of the chair next to hers and gave her a dimpled grin. She smiled in spite of herself, pleased that he'd sought her out.

"Like a baby," India answered. "You?"

"Actually, I couldn't fall asleep for some reason." Did she imagine it, or had he just winked at her?

"I finally gave up just before sunrise and went for an early run." He blew out a breath. "It was a short night."

His whiskers were more than a five-o'clock shadow today, signaling that maybe he'd been too busy to shave that morning. She wondered if they would feel softer now against her face, not that she'd minded how they'd felt last night. His hair was still damp too, with no signs of the mud he'd been hauling around for Finn.

"Yeah, I saw you out helping in the garden this morning," she blurted before she could think.

He looked surprised.

"Really? That was pretty early. You must not have slept in too late if you were up at sunrise. You should've come over and said hi. The garden is really pretty in that early-morning light. And I'm sure Finn would love to meet you."

Would he ever, Wyatt thought to himself.

India flushed. "Oh, I couldn't have. I was only in a towel. I mean . . . I was getting into the shower, but I realized I'd forgotten to turn the coffeepot off. That's when I saw the two of you."

She surely hadn't meant to make things uncomfortable, but the thought of her in only a towel was not helping his efforts to keep the conversation light this morning. He dropped his leg and cleared his throat before starting to move away.

"I suppose I should see if Vi needs anything from me before we get started. You'll love the cooking demo. The food is as beautiful to photograph as it is delicious . . ." His words trailed off as he did, and he made his way up to the front of the room, hoping she hadn't noticed that his jeans had suddenly gotten a little tighter.

He must think she was some kind of hussy. She couldn't seem to get it together around him. India was a poised, confident, educated woman, but she'd just told a guy she was crushing on that she'd watched him from her kitchen in only a towel. She squeezed her eyes shut, but as hard as she tried, she couldn't make herself disappear.

The morning flew by, and before they knew it, it was almost two o'clock. The group had just finished enjoying the lovely meal that they'd had the privilege of photographing. Shrimp and grits with a fragrant ramp pesto. Chef Mend was all about using seasonal ingredients, and while the growing season for ramps was short, they were fortunately in the middle of it now. Wyatt had unfortunately been seated between Virginia and Annabelle, the mother-daughter predators India had met the night before. He looked like a man who was waiting for a root canal; he couldn't have been more uncomfortable with their aggressive behavior.

India was sitting with Violet, who had been trying to keep her laughter in check but was failing miserably. She'd been watching Wyatt, and instead of offering him an out, she seemed to relish in his discomfort. She leaned over to India and snickered.

"Serves him right. He was annoying me at breakfast this morning, so this is his bad karma working itself out." Violet looked at India. "He was pretty tight-lipped about walking you home last night. I hope he wasn't too big of a horse's ass?"

India laughed. "No, he was great. If anything, he probably thinks I'm the one who doesn't get out much. I asked him to join me for a drink on the porch, and he practically tripped over himself trying to get out of there. I suspect he thinks I was trying to lure him inside." She cringed.

No reason to mention the rest. She didn't want to embarrass anyone, especially herself.

"So what about the kiss?" Violet asked, her eyes twinkling.

India tried not to choke on her water as she glared over at Wyatt, who was now looking back at her with a pleading look. It was obvious he wanted her to save him, but he clearly had no idea about the bomb Violet had just dropped.

Before India could answer, Violet excused herself to rush over to a stunning older woman who had just walked into the room carrying the same darling little girl from this morning. This time, India got a good look at the toddler. There was no mistaking Violet and Rex's daughter; she was a miniature version of her mother, with huge brown ringlets and a mouth full of baby teeth.

The women chatted briefly while the little girl wrapped her arms around her mother's knees. After a moment, Violet turned toward the group, asking for their attention.

"Ladies and gentlemen, we have a special treat for you today. As you may or may not know, Blackberry Farm has been owned by the same family for over forty years. The Eden family has always considered this special place their home, and everyone who comes to stay here is treated like family. We hope you've felt that way during your brief time with us so far."

She turned to the distinguished older woman next to her, who had beautiful ash-blonde hair and a slender but athletic frame draped in expensive shades of cream and white. Her twinkling eyes were an unusual gray-blue color, lending her an air of nobility, which was only reinforced by her incredible posture. India prayed she would age that beautifully.

"Please give a warm welcome to my dear friend and the proprietress of Blackberry Farm, Susan Eden."

The room erupted in warm applause, the guests clearly thrilled to be meeting one of the farm's owners. For all her wealth and privilege, Susan Eden exuded warmth, and India watched with admiration as she spoke to each of the workshop participants as if they were good friends already.

Wyatt watched Susan too, with the same jumble of feelings she always seemed to conjure up in him. He noticed that India was enchanted by her, as were most people who met her. The two women weren't that different, really. They both oozed charm and class, and both were stunningly beautiful.

He got up from his chair and made his way back over to where India was standing. She saw him coming and gave him a pointed look.

"Looks like you survived lunch without a scratch. I didn't think it was possible. I saw the claws on those two last night. Pretty fierce."

"Yeah, thanks for the heads-up. I'll have to have a discussion with Violet about her ideas on where I sit going forward. I have a feeling that suggestion wasn't an accident. Speak of the devil."

India looked up and saw Violet and Susan heading toward them. Sadie spotted Wyatt and made a run for him, leaping into his outstretched arms. She covered him in kisses as the three women looked on in amusement.

"I've always said you'd make a wonderful father, Wyatt," Susan said. "A little girl like this would just ruin you," she added with a sad smile.

Violet introduced India to Susan, and they chatted briefly before Susan moved on to greet other guests; Violet and Sadie trailing after her.

India was impressed by Susan.

"She's really something. I can't imagine the vision she and her family had to have to bring this place so far in only forty years. I heard it used to be a collection of smaller farms that the family slowly bought up over time."

She noticed that Wyatt had gone still. Looking up at him, she wondered what she'd said.

"Do you know Susan well?" she asked.

He took a breath, then released it before turning toward her and squaring his shoulders.

"I do, India. She's my mother-in-law."

CHAPTER
ELEVEN

India couldn't seem to wrap her head around that new piece of information.

He had a mother-in-law. Which meant he also had a wife.

She didn't wait for an explanation. The look on Wyatt's face told her all she needed to know.

She turned around, gathered her things, and left the barn in under a minute. He was smart enough not to try and stop her, and even had the good grace to look completely mortified as she fled.

She was glad she had the golf cart to make a quick getaway, even though Woodshed was just across the road.

Damn him. But she was mad at herself too. What the hell was she even doing? She'd jumped right out of a frying pan and into someone else's fire. She thought she was good at reading people, so it rattled her to be so off the mark with Wyatt.

And what about Violet? Why hadn't she warned India, especially since she seemed to be privy to all the scandalous details?

Something wasn't adding up, but India was too shaken to stay in the cottage, and she certainly wasn't going to be participating in any of the optional group activities scheduled for later that afternoon.

She stripped off her jeans and shirt, changing quickly into workout clothes and hiking shoes. She grabbed her camera and locked the door behind her before heading back out to the golf cart. She knew the trailhead was all the way on the other side of the Yallerhammer, and she didn't want to risk running into anyone between here and there. She needed some distance from everything and everyone. She needed to get lost.

Finn had seen India arrive just a few minutes earlier, so he was surprised when he heard the tires spin out on the gravel drive a short time later. He had glanced out the window and watched as she threw the cart back into park, ran into the house, and then came right back out again with sunglasses and workout clothes on this time. It looked like she couldn't get out of there fast enough as she veered the cart across the street and headed down the path toward the river. She had spunk, this girl. No wonder Wyatt was acting all jackrabbity. He was way out of his depth.

She was just what the doctor ordered.

Finn was cataloging some seeds a little while later when he heard voices outside his shed. Grabbing his hat off the table, he wandered outside to see what was going on.

Wyatt appeared to be standing outside the door at Woodshed, having a one-sided conversation with himself.

"India, please, I want to explain. It's not how it sounds. Just give me a minute." The boy looked pretty forlorn. Finn strolled closer and got his attention.

"She's not there. She took off like a bat outta hell a little while ago. Headed up toward the river. Way she was dressed, I expect she was meaning to find some woods."

Wyatt's disappointment was visible.

"I don't know what you did, but it can't be that bad. You two only just met. How'd you screw it up already?" Finn asked with a smile.

Wyatt ran his hands through his hair in frustration.

"She thinks I'm married, Finn. So, yeah, I'd say it's pretty bad. I doubt she'll even give me the chance to explain. She's pretty strong-willed." He paced the path, weighing his options.

"You don't say. Huh. I don't know anyone that fits that description." Finn rolled his eyes and waited for that to sink in. "Listen, you can make it right. Go find her. This is your turf; you make the rules. She'll listen if you approach her right. That is, unless you're gonna just give up. Seems to me, you might actually have a dog in this fight."

Wyatt wanted to set the record straight, that much he knew. Where they went after that was a mystery. He didn't know what the objective was for either of them, but he couldn't let her go on feeling like a fool for one minute longer. He owed her that.

He looked soberly back at Finn.

"You know, for an old guy, you're not too bad in the advice department. The delivery could use some polish, but I guess I can let it slide. Thanks, Finn."

He gave the farmer a brief hug and then ran over to the farmhouse to change his clothes before heading toward the trailhead.

India parked her cart near the small Orvis fishing shack on the banks of the river. Guests were out in droves thanks to the warm weather. India watched the choreography of the fishing lines for a moment as they danced across the surface of Hesse Creek; guests hoping to pluck trout from the rushing waters. It was perfect weather for fishing, cloudy with a chance of rain. India glanced up at the skies, confident she could get in and out of the woods before the storm.

She was just about to set out when a young guide walked out of the fishing shack.

"Just checked the radar, ma'am, and it looks like a storm is headed this way. I was just about to round everyone up off the river, so make sure that if you're headed out to hike, it's a short one." He handed her a trail map and set out to warn the other guests.

India had grabbed her rain jacket when she'd gone back to change, figuring she could use it to shelter her camera from the weather if necessary. She tied the slicker around her waist and then headed over the wooden bridge toward the trailhead. Walking along the split-rail fence that lined the property, she tried to make sense of what had just happened.

She couldn't come up with a scenario in which Wyatt could be married. Violet had flat out told her that he wasn't manipulative. How could she have possibly misunderstood that?

She reached the trailhead and, after consulting the map, decided on the longer and more challenging Trunk Branch

Trail, figuring a little rain wouldn't kill her. She needed to clear her head, and a short hike just wasn't going to cut it.

She jammed her earbuds into her ears and cranked up her music. Before she knew it, she'd been on the trail for just under an hour without running into anyone. She was drenched in sweat but felt better already. The climb had been steady, and she was high enough now to enjoy a panoramic view of the valley below. She could see the skies darkening in the west, but they didn't seem particularly ominous.

India looked through her camera's viewfinder, trying to frame a shot that would do the scene justice. She'd been distracted by the blaring music, which had driven her up the mountain but now just cluttered her senses. Removing the earbuds, she was enjoying a few moments of silence when she realized she wasn't alone.

The black bear was about two hundred yards up the trail from where India was standing. She froze in fear as the hulking creature watched her with interest, swatting at the ground in front of it in warning. She vaguely recalled the only thing she'd ever read about bear encounters, and slowly backed down the trail the way she had come. It didn't work; the creature maintained interest and began slowly moving down the path toward her.

India's body clenched in terror. She'd been just about to turn and run when she heard a commotion behind her and looked in time to see Wyatt charging by her with his arms raised over his head. The sudden movement was enough to startle the bear, and it turned and galloped back in the direction it had come. Wyatt paused, making sure he had properly spooked the animal, before turning his attention to India.

Her teeth were chattering; she was clearly in shock. He hurried back to where she stood frozen in place and pulled her into an embrace.

"It's OK. She's gone, and I doubt she's coming back."

He could feel her trembling, and he knew he had to keep talking to give her time to regain her composure.

"She probably had some cubs she was trying to protect, and you ran up on her when she wasn't expecting company."

He felt her breathing starting to return to normal, but he continued to hold her tightly against him.

"I didn't mean to scare you. Finn told me you might be headed out here, and I hoped we'd have a chance to talk."

He rubbed her back briskly and shuddered to think what might have happened if she'd been out here alone. He knew she was fiercely independent, but he instinctively found himself wanting to protect her. His arms tightened involuntarily with the realization.

India choked back the sobs that were trying to escape her. She was still in shock, but his embrace was so comforting, she felt her pulse finally start to slow. With her head against his chest, she was calmed by the rhythm of his own heartbeat. His hands were stroking her back, and despite her reservations, she allowed herself the comfort.

They quietly stood together in the woods that way for a long time, immersed in the sensation of each other's touch. It was silent except for the quiet trickle of the nearby stream and the intermittent patter of rain that had begun to fall in earnest against the canopy of leaves. It was Wyatt who finally spoke first.

"My wife died, India."

He drew a ragged breath as she pulled away from him to look into his eyes. He exhaled, relieved that he had been able to say it out loud. The entire way over to find her, he hadn't been sure how he would do it. It wasn't something he talked about with anyone; even those closest to him knew better than to bring it up.

India could see how difficult it had been for him to tell her, and she felt her heart break. Without thinking, she placed the palm of her hand against Wyatt's cheek, her other hand on his chest. Her eyes told him how sorry she was before her words could do it.

"Wyatt. No."

His eyes squeezed shut, and she dropped her hands, giving him the emotional and physical space he needed in that moment.

The rain was falling harder now, and in the distance, a rumble of thunder warned them of the gathering storm.

"We'd better head back. This forest is full of old trees, and we don't want to get caught out here if the wind starts to pick up."

Wyatt motioned for her to walk ahead of him, back toward the trailhead. As the rain fell harder, they picked up their pace, and by the time they emerged from the woods, they'd settled into a comfortable jogging rhythm side by side. They were drenched as they crossed the river, nearing the spot where India had parked her golf cart.

Wyatt had mixed feelings about having told her. The last thing he wanted was for her to pity him, but what he'd seen in her face was not what he had expected. There was something more there, something with a strong gravitational pull.

Before she could make the turn toward her cart, Wyatt grabbed her hand and led her up onto the porch of the small fishing shack that had now closed for the day because of the storm.

"Wyatt, you don't have to explain anything to me. I feel like such an ass." India stared at the ground, ashamed that she had made him get so raw. "I've spent the past two days barging into your life in every possible way, and now I've made you tell me something so deeply personal. I'm embarrassed, and I should just go back to the cottage and leave you alone."

She put her hand on top of his, patting their still clasped hands as if to say good-bye.

Wyatt pulled her close and rested his forehead against hers, their hearts both pounding now.

"Don't go, India."

He stepped back slightly to lock eyes with her, and she couldn't tell if what she saw there was pain or desire.

Or both.

CHAPTER
TWELVE

This time, there was an urgency when he kissed her, as if the frenetic energy of the storm raging around them was setting the pace.

With every clap of thunder, their kiss deepened, and before long, India found her hands wrapped around the back of his head, her fingers in his hair pulling him closer.

There were no heads involved here; this kiss was all heart. Two people realizing a chemistry that had to be explored and allowing themselves the liberty.

Wyatt had reached back and slid the ponytail out of her hair, letting it spill loose so he could weave his hands through the damp waves. He felt her breath catch as the crack of thunder sounded again, this time just overhead and loud enough to break the spell.

They reluctantly parted, and Wyatt smiled at her before turning toward the door of the shack. She watched him reach down and lift the doormat, revealing a key, which he used to open the door and go inside. He emerged a moment later holding a couple of towels and two woolen blankets. Offering a towel to India, he gestured back inside.

"We can sit out here, or if you don't mind waiting it out inside, I can fire up the weather radar and make us some coffee. There's a couple of chairs in here at least."

He was rubbing his chin with his fingers, grateful there wasn't a couch inside. He was only human, after all.

India scooped up the blankets, and they went inside together. Wyatt flipped open a laptop and fired it up to check the weather satellite, then busied himself making coffee. India dried her hair as best she could with the towel and then wove it into a loose braid to keep it off her neck. Shivering, she wrapped herself in one of the blankets and curled up in a chair. Wyatt handed her a steaming mug and then took his own chair.

The storm raged outside, and the little shack creaked and groaned in tandem with the winds. They sipped their coffee, listening as rain pelted the windows and lightning periodically lit up the cozy space.

India sighed and then quietly began speaking. "Your wife must have been pretty amazing if your mother-in-law is any indication. Susan is an incredible woman."

India didn't look at him, but she could feel his hesitation. Finally, after a few moments, he spoke. "We were very young when we got married, but we didn't have nearly enough time together."

His eyes were sad, but he had a rueful smile on his face.

"Claire and I met when we were thirteen. My parents owned the farm on the northern edge of Blackberry Farm, so we obviously went to school together. I remember seeing her get on the bus every morning and hoping she'd pick the seat next to me, which she never did."

He chuckled.

"Everyone loved Claire, and she had lots of other suitors, even at that young age, who were much braver than I was." He smiled at the memory, propping his boots out in front of him on the wooden floor.

"Do your parents still live there?" That would explain why he was always on the farm.

Wyatt stood and crossed back to the counter, adding more sugar to his coffee.

"My parents died in a car accident when I was fifteen. The Edens bought our farm after that and made it part of Blackberry. My folks hadn't put any plans in place for me in terms of guardianship, so I was set to go into foster care, but Claire stepped in and saved me."

He tapped his spoon against the mug and then walked back over to where she sat, leaning against the countertop in front of her.

"Claire only knew me as the boy from the bus, but she heard about my situation and begged her mother to adopt me. Susan was divorced from Claire's father, though, and knew she couldn't handle adding me to the mix as a single mother and the proprietress of this place."

He sat back down in his chair.

"That's when Finn stepped up and took me on as a foster kid."

India looked at him, surprised by the depth of his story. "Finn Janssen? He was your foster father?"

It was all making sense now. She thought she had noticed a special bond between the men when they were working in the garden together.

"Yep, and before long he made it official. He's an incredible man, and he's been an amazing father to me. There is nothing I wouldn't do for him."

The rain was falling softly now, but water still poured out of the overflowing gutters, trying to play catch-up. India sat in silence, marveling at what he had just told her. She waited for him to fill in the rest of his story.

"After that, Claire looked at me differently," he continued. "Most people who knew my story looked at me with pity written all over their faces. They could only see me for what I'd lost, not what remained. Claire treated me like a whole person, not damaged goods. We started hanging out together more, after school for homework, or working together with Finn in the garden. We enrolled in Violet's photo workshop together the summer after we'd both turned seventeen."

He let out a breath.

"That's when we fell in love."

Wyatt's eyes were far away as he continued.

"We made plans to apply to the same colleges and spent all of our time together that fall. It was just before Christmas when she got sick. That damned tumor was relentless. Everything we did to fight it seemed to just make it stronger. Doctors gave her less than a year to live, but we prayed for a miracle every day."

Tears shimmered in India's eyes, and she had to stop herself from reaching for him, halted by the naked grief on his face.

"By the next summer, we knew we wouldn't get that miracle. I loved her so much, and knew that I wanted to spend the time we had left together in a meaningful way. Susan gave us her blessing, and we married that fall. She was my wife for only three weeks, but I carry her spirit with me still today. She saved me, but I couldn't save her."

India was weeping softly for Claire—and for Wyatt and Susan whom she'd left behind. And for the power of the love she felt pouring forth from this beautiful man who had privately carried this story in his heart for so many years. She felt honored that he'd felt safe enough to share it with her.

They were both startled to hear the sounds of heavy boots out on the porch, and they watched as the door opened and Finn poked his head inside. Relief washed over his face when he saw the two of them, followed by a flustered expression in response to walking in on an obviously charged moment.

"Oh good, just making sure you two didn't go out to take a walk and the hogs ate you," he joked. "That was some storm. Saw some downed trees on the way over; I might need a hand with those in the next couple of days if you have time, Wyatt."

Finn shot a bashful smile at India and tipped his hat to her.

"Finn Janssen, ma'am. I think we're neighbors this week, if you're staying over in Woodshed."

India rose and offered her hand, smiling warmly at this man who had given so much to Wyatt.

"I'm India, and, yes . . . I am staying in Woodshed. I'd love to come over and take a look at your seeds if you have some time to spare. I'm so grateful for the work you do to preserve heirloom plants."

"That's mighty kind of you, India. Pleased to make your acquaintance. Stop by anytime, and we'll have a chat and a stroll through the garden," Finn said.

He nodded over to where Wyatt was standing.

"Be best if Wyatt here drives you back. There are several blocked paths that we'll need to clear, but looks like the next few days are gonna be beauties, so that's good."

Finn walked over and slapped Wyatt on the back, telling him the way that was clear to go back, and waved at them both as he lumbered out the door and off the porch.

India stood and folded the blanket, handing it back to Wyatt. She rounded up their mugs and took a moment to wash them in the sink, leaving them upside down to dry. Wyatt turned the computer off, and they locked up, placing the key back where they'd found it.

They were quiet most of the way back to her place. They'd just passed the dairy building when Wyatt got up the nerve to say, "I want to take you on a date."

He looked straight ahead as he said it, but a smile crept across his face when he felt her eyes on him.

"That probably sounds lame, but I'm not sure how else to let you know that I like you, and I figure I'd better stop kissing you so much before I at least treat you to dinner."

India laughed out loud before she could help herself.

"I'd love to have dinner with you," she said. "But only if you promise there'll be more kissing after."

She couldn't believe her own courage, proud of herself for being so bold.

He burst out with a laugh of his own.

"I guess that could be arranged," he said.

He pulled the cart up to the foot of the path and turned to face her again. "How about I pick you up tomorrow night after class, around six thirty? I know it's a little early, but I want to show you something." He gave her that dimpled grin.

She nodded with a smile. "Now you've piqued my curiosity. I'll be ready. And, Wyatt, thanks again for today. For everything."

India leaned over and gave him a kiss on the cheek, hopped out of the cart, and headed into her cottage.

CHAPTER
THIRTEEN

India's phone was ringing when she got out of the shower the next morning. She'd taken extra time, shaving her legs and deep-conditioning her hair, thinking about their upcoming date. Hurriedly wrapping herself in a towel, she grabbed her phone off the counter and answered it just in time. It was Julia, full of questions.

"Oh good, I thought I was gonna miss you again. How was your day? Did you end up going to that workshop? I figured you must have, since I kept getting your voice mail."

India smiled and put her friend on speakerphone so she could start brushing through her hair while they talked.

"Sorry, Jules. Yeah, I went, and I left my phone back here plugged in. I went out for a hike afterward and forgot to grab it."

She skipped the part about the bear encounter, instead asking Jules about Pearl. She was relieved to hear that the little girl seemed to be getting over the flu, but it sounded like they were in it for the long haul with the chicken pox. India laughed when Jules described how glamorous her last for-ty-eight hours had been, on duty and covered in vomit while Mike slept peacefully in the guest room so he "didn't disturb her."

"I swear, my thirty-five-year-old is the problem child. The other two are easy," Julia joked, and India laughed because she knew Jules was including the family dog in the easy group.

India smoothed some lotion onto her legs and changed the subject.

"So, I have a date tonight, Jules." She smiled as her friend fired off a string of when, where, why, and how questions.

"It's actually the guy from the airport. He lives here, and he's helping teach part of the photography class, so we've got-ten to know each other a little better over the past couple of days."

She realized she'd been trailing her fingertips along her collarbone while she spoke of Wyatt, and she felt a bloom of desire at the thought of his hands in her hair yesterday, remov-ing her ponytail. She'd wear it down tonight. Save a step.

She sat down at the small illuminated vanity, taking her time with some light makeup. She shouldn't have bothered packing her blush on this trip, although the fact that the NARS color she'd brought with her was called Orgasm didn't escape her.

"So tell me about him," Julia asked, and then listened as India filled her in on what Wyatt had shared yesterday. Her friend was quiet as India retold Wyatt's story and then described Violet and Rex, and Finn and Susan. Julia was thoughtful with her response, only speaking when India finished.

"I haven't heard you like this before, Indy," said Julia, using her friend's childhood nickname. "At least not for a long time. You sound so different than you did even a few days ago. Are you sure you know what you're doing? Getting involved with a widower is pretty deep, although he does sound amazing. I just don't want you to get hurt again."

India had been awake much of the night thinking these same thoughts, but had come to the conclusion that she couldn't imagine not exploring whatever this was with Wyatt. It was something cosmic, something she couldn't ignore.

"I'm alright, Jules. I know what I'm doing. If you met him, you'd understand. He's so different than anyone I've ever known. Besides, it's just dinner," she added, even though India suspected that was definitely an understatement.

Wyatt did his best to concentrate on the photography that afternoon in class, but he found his mind wandering to thoughts of that evening. He knew he was opening up to the possibility of being hurt again, falling for this woman who was leaving at the end of the week, but he couldn't help himself.

He was quietly watching her again as Rex showed her how to use some of her camera equipment more thoroughly, intrigued by her obvious talent for photography. He was wondering why she hadn't pursued it as a career, when Violet sidled up next to him, elbowing him gently in the side.

"Someone's smitten, huh?" she asked with a grin. "I told you to give her a chance. She's something special, Wyatt . . . it's just a feeling I have."

Wyatt gave her a sideways look, letting out a sigh and turning his attention to the PowerPoint presentation he would finish up the workshop with.

"As much as it pains me to admit it, you're right, Vi. She's really something. I told her everything—about Claire and Finn."

He looked at Violet, more vulnerable than he'd felt in a long time.

"I'm taking her up to the ridge tonight. It's the first time I've shared that with anyone."

He searched Violet's face for approval and found it as her eyes filled with tears.

"Oh, Wyatt, you don't know how happy that makes me. I know it's hard to move forward, even after all this time, but it's what Claire would have wanted, and you know that Susan only wants for you to be happy. It's time for you to start living again."

She grabbed him in an impulsive hug as she discreetly brushed the tears from her eyes.

"Don't worry about what the future holds, Wyatt. The two of you met for a reason, so explore that and see where it takes you. Remember, you can't push the river."

Wyatt supposed she was right, but it still terrified him to think about where this was headed. What scared him even more was the fact that he had no desire to change course. He was going for it, and he felt himself feeling hopeful for the first time in recent memory.

Wyatt stopped on the way to India's cottage to pick a handful of delicate pink and white mountain laurels. The warmer weather had the fields awash with the spring blooms, and Wyatt suspected she would love them. He wore an olive-green button-down over a brown T-shirt, with jeans and boots. He'd mentioned to her that they would go casual for dinner, and he couldn't wait to see her interpretation.

He had never shared this much of his life with a woman, so he was understandably nervous as he pulled up to Woodshed in Olive. He was just getting out of the truck and heading to the door when she opened it and stepped outside.

His heart skipped a beat. She was wearing a flowing blue sundress with a white denim jacket rolled at the sleeves and flat sandals. Her hair was loose around her shoulders in waves. She smiled shyly and headed down the path toward him.

Wyatt couldn't speak, so he was glad when she did.

"They're lovely. Are they for me?" she asked, gesturing toward the flowers in his hand.

He'd forgotten he was even holding them, and they suddenly looked less special next to her.

"Yes, I picked them for you on the way over. The wildflowers are just starting to fill up the meadows; I'll drive by and show you where I got them on our way."

He smiled and handed the petite bouquet to India.

"They're nowhere near as beautiful as you are, though," he told her.

She blushed then, taking the flowers back inside to find a vase, leaving him waiting by his truck.

While she was inside, Wyatt glanced over and saw Finn walking out of the garden shed, closing it up for the evening. Finn noticed Wyatt waiting there and raised his hand in a silent wave, flashing his son a toothy grin. He couldn't resist a thumbs-up before turning to head home.

India had come back outside and was locking up the cottage. They walked to Olive, and Wyatt held her door for her as she gathered her skirt and climbed up into the truck.

He took a deep breath and then exhaled before climbing into the driver's seat. The sun had just set, and dusk was settling over the gardens, bathing everything in a warm glow. He started the truck and they headed down the road, back in the direction of where they'd gone hiking the day before.

"Where are we going?" India asked him as they drove down the familiar road. "Not back into bear country, I hope," she joked with a smile.

Wyatt laughed. "You'll see. I want to show you a place that's special to me. It's just up here, on the other side of the chapel."

India had seen the small church on her way to the trail-head the day before, but she'd noticed a private property sign and figured it was reserved for the use of the family. They drove up over one final hill and around a wooded bend to a clearing in the woods.

Sitting there in the opening was a silver Airstream trailer strung with white lights. Under the canopy was a small table for two, set for dinner. A grill stood off to one side, and a small bonfire was ready to be lit. The sky was indigo now, and the twinkling lights made it all seem like a dream. It was the most romantic setting India had ever seen. Wyatt smiled at her reaction and put the truck in park.

"Welcome to my home," he said to her with a smile.

CHAPTER

FOURTEEN

They got out of the truck, and Wyatt took her by the hand, leading her to the campsite. He'd obviously come up here earlier to get everything ready, because she could hear the music as they got closer and saw that he had some beer and a bottle of wine chilling in a bucket near the table.

"This place is amazing," she told him, rubbing his hand in hers. "You live here?"

Wyatt kissed her hand before letting it go, busying himself with lighting the bonfire.

"Not exactly. Well, sometimes. This is a part of my family's original farm. Susan was kind enough to deed me this land when I turned twenty-one, with hopes that I would one day build a home here so we could remain close. I guess she figures I'm taking my sweet time making that happen."

He sat back and watched the flames lick the firewood, catching and creating a blaze. She observed his face bathed in firelight as he grew quiet.

"Susan is the closest thing to a mother that I've got. She's been like a parent to me, along with Finn, and I know she'd love nothing more than for me to build on this site and start a family here. I would never intentionally hurt her, but the closest I've come is parking this Airstream here instead of building something more permanent. Every time I leave, I know she wonders if I'll be coming back, and it kills me to do that to her."

Wyatt stood up then, brushing small flakes of ash from his thighs, and turned his attention back to India.

"I'm thinking it might be time now to consider putting down some roots. Violet and Rex will be gone for the year, so I'm stuck here anyway. Might as well build something with better plumbing," he added, his eyes twinkling.

India smiled at that, grabbing both of his hands in hers.

"Thank you for bringing me here. This place is really special. If you build, I hope you'll still keep the Airstream here. It's amazing, and very romantic, I must say." She reached up and kissed his cheek quickly before pulling away to create some space between them. "Wait, I forgot; no kissing before dinner." She laughed. "What can I do to help?"

Wyatt had to order himself not to grab her right then and carry her inside; instead, he asked her to grab the steaks from the fridge. He went to work lighting the grill and then poured her a glass of wine, popping open a beer for himself.

India stepped inside the trailer, glancing around at the living space. This was no ordinary Airstream. With a leather banquette and hardwood floors, it looked like it had been decked out by a professional. The walls were a warm squash color, lending a masculine but welcoming feeling to the space.

She could see a bed in the rear and imagined him sleeping out here alone. The thought made her sad. She noticed a few prints on the walls and wondered if they were his own work.

After grabbing the steaks she stepped back outside, where Wyatt was busy with the grill. She laid the steaks on the table beside it. They chatted about that day's class, settling into comfortable conversation while the meat sizzled away.

India wandered out to the edge of the site and looked up at the sky, which was dotted once again with stars. The food smelled delicious, and she took a moment to close her eyes and soak it all in. This was so different from her life back home, but she was so at peace here. She felt bad about her past disdain for all things rural. It had come from a place of fear, she realized. Fear of the unknown. Now here she was, as uncertain about her life as she'd ever been, yet she felt strangely content about it all.

Wyatt announced that dinner was ready, so they sat down at the small table together and tucked in to the delicious meal.

Wyatt had watched her standing under the stars and wondered what she was thinking about. He decided it was time to hear her story.

"Tell me about your life in New York," he said, topping off her wineglass and grabbing another beer for himself. He was surprised when she hesitated.

"Manhattan is fine. It's nothing like this, though. I've only lived there for less than two years; I relocated for my job," she told him, sipping her wine and gathering the courage to tell him about her life.

"What do you do?" he asked her, sensing she was afraid to talk about it.

"I work in television, actually. I'm a reporter and anchor on the *Today* show, at NBC."

She watched that sink in, his surprised expression confirming that he really had had no idea. She willed herself to tell him the rest. He had shared so much with her; it was only fair that she do the same.

"I'm taking some time off now because of personal stuff that happened several months ago."

Wyatt watched her and waited for her to tell him the rest.

"I told you I was supposed to get married and that I couldn't go through with it, but I didn't mention that I made that decision on our wedding day. I said yes when I should've said no, and I got swept up in it all. For the longest time, I couldn't figure out how to stop it, but fortunately, I found my voice at the last minute."

She couldn't meet his eyes but continued on in a rush, anxious to get it all out there.

"My ex-fiancé is the meteorologist at another network, and there was a bit of an uproar about my getting cold feet, so it was suggested that I take some time off until the whole thing blows over." She smiled meekly and drained her wineglass. Setting it down, she added, "So here I am, out of sight and out of mind."

Wyatt considered what she'd told him. It was obviously painful for her to talk about, and he appreciated her honesty. He felt like an ass for not knowing who she was, but then why would he? He didn't even own a TV.

"What was it that made you call it off? Was it marriage or was it the guy?" He stood up to stoke the fire, noticing she was shivering a bit, either from nerves or from the night air.

She answered quickly. "I think it was a little of both. Jack definitely wasn't the guy for me, I'm sure of that. But I've always believed that my life needed to go according to some grand plan I made years ago, and I guess I finally realized that I have to be open to making adjustments when needed.

Who knows if I'll even be welcomed back to work after this. Viewers are fickle. They might decide I'm not what they want since I blew up their idea of a fairy tale."

Wyatt thought about everything she'd said. He could relate. For so long, he'd resigned himself to the fact that he would live alone. He didn't want anyone in his life. He could see the value now in making adjustments to that stupid plan. He sat back down across from her.

"I think it's brave what you did, but I think you're being a little hard on yourself," he said. "We all have ideas of the way we want things to go, but, as John Lennon said, 'Life is what happens to you while you're busy making other plans.'" He gave her a rueful smile. "I never expected to make my life here in Walland after Claire died," Wyatt continued. "But it's funny how things can change when you least expect it."

They looked at each other over the forgotten dinner plates for a moment before Wyatt rose and reached for her hand.

"Dance with me," he said.

India stood and allowed him to pull her slowly toward him. She rested her head on his shoulder, one arm around him, her other hand in his. They swayed to the strains of Van Morrison's "Into the Mystic," both relieved to have shared their stories.

It was just the two of them in that moment, everything else forgotten. They stayed that way until the song was finished and was replaced by a John Mayer tune. India lifted her head and looked at Wyatt quizzically.

"How about that kiss you promised me?" she asked, her eyes serious this time.

Wyatt couldn't help himself. He thrust his hands into her hair and crushed his mouth to hers. It felt like coming home after a long time gone. He'd been craving the taste of her all day, and it was better than he'd remembered. His desire for her was obvious as they stumbled backward together toward the Airstream.

Wyatt placed his hand behind her head to cushion the blow as he pressed her urgently up against the body of the trailer so he could get better leverage. He couldn't get close enough, and something inside warned him to stop, but he didn't listen. He was physically unable.

She could feel that he wanted her, and she couldn't stop herself from shifting her position and grinding her hips to match his. She heard him groan and felt her stomach flutter. He was so unbelievably sexy; she couldn't seem to maintain control. His hands started to explore, running down her arms and grasping her hands for a moment, before traveling back up her rib cage and grazing the sides of her breasts.

Her sharp intake of breath at that touch was enough to snap him back to reality. He didn't want to take things too far before the time was right. He couldn't risk losing her. He was falling fast, and that realization made him pull back and take a step away from her.

"I think we'd better get you home. I want a shot at another date, and if we don't leave now, this one might never end." He ran his fingers through his hair and distracted himself with stacking their dishes and taking them inside.

India was trying her best to regain composure, smoothing her own hair back into submission and pulling her jacket back up over her shoulders. She wasn't sure what she'd done to make him stop, but she wasn't going to settle for this. She helped him finish clearing the dishes and thanked him for the evening.

On the drive home, she knew what she had to do.

They arrived back at Woodshed, and Wyatt came around the car to walk India to the door. He stepped back to say good night, and she made her move.

"You're going to have that drink with me tonight, and I won't take no for an answer." She saw him hesitate, so she grabbed his hand to reassure him.

"Here's the catch: I forgot to get bourbon today, so can you run over to the barn and grab us a bottle?"

Wyatt knew he was taking a risk by agreeing, but looking at her, he couldn't say no.

"OK. I'll run over and find some. Be back in a few."

India smiled and went inside the cottage, leaving the screen door unlocked for him.

Wyatt crossed the road to the barn and tried not to break into a run. He wanted her, but he was trying to be a gentleman so she wouldn't get spooked. Maybe I underestimated her, he thought as he waited for the staff to bring him a bottle of Basil Hayden's up from storage.

He grabbed two rocks glasses and filled them with ice before heading back across the street. He prayed she hadn't change her mind in the fifteen minutes he'd been gone. He heard music as he knocked gently before pushing the door open with his knee.

The room was dark, except for candlelight. She wasn't in the main room, he noticed as he glanced around. He saw that the bathroom door was ajar, and he could hear that the music was coming from inside.

He heard her voice call out softly to him.

"Come in, Wyatt," she said.

He still had his hands full with the bourbon and glasses, so he used his elbow to nudge the bathroom door open a little farther.

He froze in place.

She was sitting in a steaming tub full of bubbles, her hair in a loose topknot. The room flickered with candlelight, and he could see her clothes in a heap on the floor where she'd stepped out of them. Norah Jones was asking someone to come away with her.

India asked him something else altogether.

"Take a bath with me, Wyatt."

CHAPTER
FIFTEEN

He was dumbstruck. She was a vision, and she was inviting him into a dream. She sat in an oversized claw-foot tub, which was centered in the middle of the room between two windows. She'd lined the sills with tea lights, and, if the empty container beside her was any indication, she'd added bourbon-vanilla bubble bath to the tub.

He somehow figured out how to control his body again.

Their eyes locked on each other; he moved to the vanity and poured them a drink to share. He set the glass on a small table next to the tub. Leaning over her, so their faces were just inches apart, he spoke for the first time since entering the room.

"Are you sure, India?" he said, his voice tortured. His features were stone, but the raw desire in his eyes was unmistakable.

"I'm sure," she said, straining up toward him to get close enough to rub her nose against his. Fire erupted in him.

He kicked off his boots and shrugged out of his button-down, all the while maintaining her gaze. He recognized the craving in her eyes, and it fueled him as he picked up the pace, lifting his T-shirt up and over his head.

India was mesmerized. He was incredible-looking. His torso had a light smattering of dark hair that disappeared into a V at his waistband. She was shaking under the water, but she couldn't let him know it. She'd realized that she would have to make the first move with him if they were ever going to quit wasting their short time together. She shuddered with anticipation as he stepped out of his jeans and, wearing only his boxer briefs, walked around to the back of the tub, removing those too, before climbing in and sliding down behind her.

The sensation of him was electrifying, but he teased her with his leisurely pace. Instead of touching her, he reached over and brought the glass of bourbon to her lips. She sipped the drink, letting it burn a trail through her insides. He took a drink himself, then returned the glass to the table.

She worked up the courage to run her hands up and down his legs, which were wrapped around her, and they tightened in response to her touch. He swept a few loose tendrils of her hair to the side and placed a tender kiss where her neck and shoulder met, causing her to shudder.

She leaned her head back and lost herself in the feel of him. His hands reached down to hold hers under the water, and they lay together, their hearts beating in tandem for a while.

Time passed, although they weren't sure how much. Coldplay's "Fix You" came on, and Wyatt began a leisurely exploration, starting with his splayed palms against her belly. She quivered as he journeyed upward, cupping her breasts gently before allowing his fingers to graze her nipples. She arched back at the contact, rotating her body just enough to look at him, and then began a tour of his chest with her own hands.

Wyatt had done his best up to that point to let her take the lead, but her slippery touch in the water pushed him into sensory overload. In one swift move, he pivoted her across his lap, so that they were now facing each other in the mound of suds, their legs intertwined, but the rest of them once again independent of each other. He gazed at her in awe, and a thousand things were said between them without words. She raised her hand to his cheek, wiping off the bubbles that had landed there. He grabbed her hand, kissing each of her fingertips, before laying that hand back against his chest. He finally found the words.

"India, my heart is pounding out of my chest, and I promise you it's nothing that bourbon can fix. God help me, but I want you more than I've ever wanted anything in my life. Please let me take you to bed."

He waited for her, watching for the answer. She didn't speak but rose from the tub and offered him her hand. He stepped out onto the slate floor and waited for her to do the same before wrapping her up in a fluffy white towel. Swathing his own hips in a second towel, he followed her out into the bedroom. She turned to face him, letting her towel drop to the floor.

"I want to look at you, Wyatt, and I want you to see me. All of me. I don't know what's happened, but I feel like I'm under your spell."

He inhaled deeply, letting his towel fall to meet hers, showing her just how captivated he was by her.

She let her gaze travel over him. He was magnificent. Wyatt couldn't wait a moment longer. He stepped toward her and scooped her up, and with two confident strides, he set her tenderly on the bed before him.

She reached her arms above her head, stretching like a cat as he started the trail of kisses at her ankles and worked his way up. When he reached her center, he rose up to look at her, waiting once again for her permission. She looked down at him with a smoky glance and nodded the smallest of affirmations. He didn't hesitate.

She'd never known it was possible to experience pure bliss this way; the lovers that had come before him weren't in his league. When he was certain she'd peaked, he rose up again to look at her, surprised to see her eyes closed, a single tear running down her cheek.

Wyatt panicked, sliding himself up next to her. He brought her face to his in a kiss before nuzzling her into his chest protectively. "I'm sorry, India. I couldn't help myself."

She lifted her face to him and stopped his words with a kiss, deepening the contact of their bodies. She reached down to stroke him, and he groaned as their mouths parted. Rolling him over onto his back, she dusted him with kisses, maintaining the rhythm she'd started. When it was clear he was at the edge, she lowered herself onto him, her hands on his chest and their eyes on each other the entire time.

They began to move together, their tempo in sync from the start. A million thoughts ran through India's head, but she wasn't able to grasp any of them. Her body was in complete control now. Or, at least, she thought so. Wyatt had other ideas.

He pulled her face down toward his, flipping her over onto her back while he was still inside her, and nudged his head into her neck, placing almost-painless biting kisses there. Their pace quickened again, and after a time, India cried out his name. That was enough. He never wanted to hear his name cross another woman's lips again.

The climax was shattering, and like everything else, they were perfectly in sync. Wyatt's mind was racing too, but one thought rang clear and true: he was falling in love with her.

The night was quiet except for the sounds of the outdoors floating in. India lay next to Wyatt, watching his chest rise and fall with each breath. He looked peaceful in his sleep, more boy than man, which made her smile. He was a rare find, and she felt a rising panic when she thought of leaving him. Of leaving this place. She instinctively snuggled in closer to him, breathing in his scent. She'd bottle it to have forever if she could.

She closed her eyes again, and for the first time in a long time, her sleep was dreamless.

CHAPTER
SIXTEEN

Sunlight was streaming through the windows when Wyatt awoke. It took him a moment to figure out where he was, but once he did, his body responded instantly to the memory of the night before. He stretched, reaching for her, but found the bed empty. He propped himself up on one elbow, vaguely aware of the smell of coffee. Feeling a cool breeze, he looked over and saw that it was coming from the open door leading out onto the screened-in porch.

He climbed out of bed and headed into the bathroom to find his jeans on the floor where he'd left them. After slipping them on, he reached over and pulled the drain to empty the water from the tub. He splashed some water on his face and used the complimentary toothbrush and paste before padding barefoot out onto the enclosed porch.

India was standing at the screen in a white robe, looking out at the garden, her hands clasped around a steaming mug of coffee. He couldn't get over how lovely she was; her spirit was both strong and gentle, and he once again felt the gravitational pull. She must have felt it too, because she glanced over her shoulder, as if she knew he'd been there watching her, and treated him again to that beautiful blush. He hoped she never found a way to control it.

"It's about time," India said with a shy smile as Wyatt took her coffee mug and set it on the ledge, before wrapping his arms around her from behind. "I was just about to come back in there and check for a pulse." She shivered as she felt him inhaling her scent as he nuzzled her hair. "Did you sleep well?"

He took her by the shoulders, turning her toward him before wrapping her in his arms and pulling her in against his chest.

He was still warm from the bed. India couldn't believe how sexy he looked in those unbuttoned jeans and bare feet. His hair was damp from his cursory stop at the sink, and his face was darkened by two days' worth of stubble. He was dreamy. If she didn't know better, she'd think he was trying to get her to skip class. She waited for him to answer her, enjoying the intimacy of her cheek against his bare chest.

"I haven't slept like that in years. Morning sure got here quick, though." She felt him laugh, and raised her head to look at him.

He smiled at her then before his face grew serious. The fire between them was still there; last night had done nothing to extinguish it. In fact, it was even more powerful now, if that was possible. But there was also a sense of desperation. It felt as if someone had turned an hourglass upside down, and the sands were running through at an alarming pace. They were aware that they had only a few days left together, and neither of them intended to waste a second.

Wyatt took a ragged breath and started to speak, but before he could, she took his face in her hands and kissed him. This time, it was slow, leisurely, and filled with all that was still unspoken between them. She tasted of coffee and all that was good about mornings. He released his hold on her and slipped his hands inside her robe, wrapping them around her, feeling her soft bare skin tingle with goose bumps.

She nudged him backward, and they stepped over the threshold and into the bedroom, never breaking contact. She unbuttoned his jeans and slid them down his legs, and he hurriedly stepped out of them. India shrugged out of her robe, letting it drop to the floor behind her, as their hands urgently roamed the landscapes of each other, the heat between them reaching a feverish pitch now.

India had seen his expression on the porch, and it frightened her. She felt this thing between them too, but it was easier to speak like this, to let their bodies do the talking. She was completely enraptured by him but had no idea where this would lead.

For once in her life, she was choosing to travel without a map, and it was terrifying and thrilling at the same time.

Summoning up her last bit of confidence, she pulled away from him and, grabbing his hand, led him into the bathroom, where she reached in and started the shower. She'd planned to wait for the water to heat up, but it was evidently plumbed to instantly run hot, the steam forming in the chilly room almost immediately.

Wyatt followed her in, closing the door behind them as he bowed his head to bite the back of her neck again, just as he'd done the night before in the tub. He knew how she would respond.

The effect was sensational, and she gasped and reached out, splaying her palms against the fogged-up shower glass.

Seeing her like that in front of him, it took everything he had not to take her from behind. The sway of her body as she arched her head back toward him made her look irresistible. He summoned a shred of composure, pulling her around to face him before meeting her lips with his. He didn't know what was making it so hard to breathe—the steam, the kiss, or the woman. He couldn't wait another minute to have her again. He reached down, sliding himself inside of her, and they clung to each other, moving together in this world they had created until they finally shattered back down to earth, suddenly feeling like two halves of a whole.

Finn was laying out the day ahead in his journal as he always did, when he saw Wyatt and India kissing good-bye outside her door. He'd seen the truck parked there when he'd arrived at his garden shed that morning and had smiled to himself. The boy was finally ready to start living again, and Finn couldn't be happier. It killed him to think that Wyatt could end up old and alone like he'd been for most of his life now. Wyatt had so much to share with someone, if he could just allow himself the chance to be happy again.

He watched as Wyatt bounded down the path to his truck, chuckling to himself at the noticeable spring in the boy's step. Must've been one hell of a date, but then Finn had figured it would be when he'd heard Wyatt's plans to take her up to the ridge. Finn knew what that land meant to Wyatt, and he understood how important it was that the boy had chosen to share it with India. It was a good sign.

He'd been mortified when he'd interrupted them at the fishing shack the other day. It was clear they'd been having a deep conversation of some kind, because there was a spark in

Wyatt's eyes that Finn hadn't noticed since Claire. He prayed that India understood how meaningful this was; Finn was hopeful that it was mutual, since he'd noticed the raw emotion on India's face when he'd barged in on them. He figured Wyatt must have shared everything with her.

Finn supposed he'd better find time to have a chat with the girl himself before the week got away from them all. He knew better than most that love could be both precious and fragile, and you needed to seize it when it crossed your path. For however long you could. He'd gladly do his part to help these two kids along.

Violet had seen Wyatt's truck outside of Woodshed too. She'd been enjoying her own cup of coffee, perusing the day's newsletter that outlined the farm's schedule of activities, when she heard a car door slam. She'd stepped out onto the back porch in time to see Wyatt's truck pull away from the cottage, and she'd known instantly that he hadn't been there to borrow a cup of sugar. She'd seen Olive parked there when she'd gone to bed the night before and had made a mental note to grill Wyatt about the date today. Now she couldn't wait to get to class.

She rinsed her coffee cup and locked the back door before heading back upstairs. Sadie was still sleeping when she peeked in on her, so Violet knew she had a few more minutes before they had to start getting ready.

Tiptoeing into the master suite, she slipped off her robe and crawled back into bed. Wrapping her arms around Rex, she kissed his shoulder to rouse him from a deep sleep. She rubbed her feet against the warmth of his legs, grateful for these last few moments of quiet together.

It wasn't long before Rex rolled over to face Violet, still amazed—as he was every day—that he got to wake up next to this gorgeous creature. It was especially wonderful when she was clearly trying to get his attention, which she definitely was now. He could see from her expression, though, that she had something to tell him, so he gave up, sighed, and folded his arms behind his head, knowing she wouldn't even consider anything else until she'd unburdened herself.

"I don't know for sure, but I think Wyatt spent the night with India," she told him excitedly. "I just saw him leaving, and I know for a fact he was still there when we went to bed last night. What do you think we should do? Can we invite them to join us for dinner at that celebrity-chef thingy tonight at the barn? I'm *dying* to see them together."

Rex knew how important it was to Violet that Wyatt find happiness again. Seeing his friend with India, it was the first time he'd believed his wife might get her wish. It sure would make Violet feel less guilty about stranding Wyatt here at the farm while they took off to travel the world.

Violet was still trying to figure out ways to fan the flames, and she would have kept right on scheming, but Rex laughed and pulled his wife over on top of him, pushing her hair back away from her face. He loved her more now than on the day they'd married, and her concern for others was one of his favorite things about her. That and her incredible body.

"Dinner sounds great; let's start there. You can plan the wedding later." He stroked her cheek tenderly. "But right now, enough about Wyatt and India, and forget about dinner. I'm fixing to have something even better for breakfast. It's official. I'm hot for teacher," he joked, knowing they'd have to hurry if they didn't want to be late for class.

CHAPTER
SEVENTEEN

India was about to turn the blow-dryer on when she noticed her phone lighting up on the vanity. Julia was FaceTiming her. She grabbed the device and took a deep breath before answering. Her friend's face popped up on the screen, and they both grinned, happy to see each other as always. India spoke first.

"I'm *so* sorry I've been out of touch, Jules! The service here is so spotty, and I've been out and about at classes and stuff. I should have checked in. How's Pearl? Please tell me the worst is over," India begged.

Jules stared at her friend on the screen for a moment before answering.

"Pearl is fine; we've turned the corner. No more flu, so now we just have to wait out the chicken pox." She paused, a funny look on her face as she continued. "What's wrong with you? Why do you look so different?"

Julia saw the blush creek up India's neck and gasped.

"You'd better start talking right now. That must have been some first date! Holy shit . . . tell me everything."

India knew she couldn't hide anything from Jules, and it would feel really good to talk about Wyatt with her. She filled her friend in on finding out about Claire and meeting Wyatt's mother-in-law, and about their date out at the Airstream. She hesitated for a moment, not sure how to explain the rest. India wasn't sure what was happening herself. But if she looked different, it was for good reason. She certainly felt different.

"He's amazing, Jules. He's smart and funny, and I mean . . . sexy doesn't even begin to cover it." India closed her eyes, the image of him making her a little weak. "I let myself get carried away." India smiled sheepishly at Julia's stunned expression and added, "Twice, actually. So far."

She covered her mouth as Jules's jaw dropped open.

"Oh my God, no wonder you've been MIA! So what's the deal with this guy? Why do I get the feeling this is more than a fling for you? I haven't seen you like this since . . . well . . . ever. What are you going to do when you have to go back to work?"

Julia was pacing now, and India could see her friend trying to rationalize the situation as she fired questions at her.

"I don't even know what we're doing, Jules, I can't explain. It's like this weird magnetism, and we can't seem to stay away from each other. The sex is off the charts. I mean, it's curl-your-toes amazing." India let out a frustrated breath. "It's more than that, though. He's deep, Julia. When he looks at me, it's like he really sees who I am, maybe even better than I see myself."

India glanced at the clock, realizing she'd better throw her hair in a braid and wrap things up if she were going to get to the workshop on time.

"For once in my life, I'm just going with the flow. Is that crazy?" she asked her friend.

Julia was standing still now, riveted by the look on her friend's face. She grinned at India and shook her head in disbelief.

"I don't think it's crazy at all, but I can't believe I'm hearing you say these things. You of all people. Don't get me wrong. I think it's great, and I vote for lots more toe curling this week. And job, schmob. Wasn't it Scarlett O'Hara who said, 'After all, tomorrow is another day'? Come to think of it, she lost both guys, so maybe that's not a great example." They laughed together.

India could hear Pearl just then, calling for her mama, so she blew them both a kiss and said good-bye, promising to call Julia in the next day or so. She grabbed her camera bag and ran out the door to head to class with just five minutes to spare.

When India walked into the barn, Wyatt was standing up at the front preparing for his presentation, but he wasn't alone.

Virginia, the man-eating daughter from Atlanta, was leaning suggestively against the counter in front of him, her fitted blouse providing an ample representation of what she could offer him. Wyatt was trying to answer her question in earnest, but he was obviously working hard to keep his eyes north of the spectacle before him. There was enough cleavage on display that India almost wanted to drop a quarter between her breasts to see if a song would play.

India found a chair and was hanging her purse on the arm of it when she saw Violet approaching her. *Game face,* she told herself. She knew Wyatt wouldn't have had the time to talk with his friends yet today, and she sure wasn't going to be the first to provide any details. She smiled warmly at Violet and decided to go on the offensive.

"Hey, Violet. I'm excited for class today. Wyatt's doing his presentation on landscape, right?"

Perfect, she thought, *keep it all business. Don't show your hand.*

"He is, and I'm sure he's ready to get started as soon as Betty Boop takes her seat."

They laughed, watching as Virginia left to find her mother, realizing her efforts to captivate Wyatt were probably in vain. Violet turned her attention back to India.

"Rex and I are attending a private event tonight down in the wine cellar. A celebrity chef is preparing the meal, then speaking about her inspiration afterward. We'd love it if you and Wyatt could join us? Finn will be there too, and Susan Eden. It's a cool experience to have dinner downstairs, so please say yes."

She waited expectantly for India to answer her, but before she could, India heard Wyatt answer over her shoulder.

"We'd love to." He looked at India. "That is, if it's OK with you?" He relaxed when she nodded in agreement, smiling as she looked up at him. "How thoughtful of you to invite us, Vi." Wyatt was now eying Violet suspiciously, who just smiled sweetly back at him.

He knew what she was up to, but he wouldn't pass up the chance to spend more time with India, even if it meant being subjected to Violet's firing squad.

"Great. There's a cocktail reception first, out on the patio. Meet us there at seven? As long as that gives you two enough time for . . . whatever your afternoon plans are?"

She looked innocently between them, ignoring Wyatt's glare.

"Sounds perfect," said India as Violet pivoted toward the front of the room, heading to the podium to begin the workshop.

Wyatt turned to her, his voice low. "I don't know how I'm going to stand up there and teach when all I want to do is find a dark corner and devour you again."

His eyes were opaque, and he gave her a wolfish grin, brushing his hand against hers as he turned to meet Violet at the front of the class. She'd had the very same thought that morning. The touch was fleeting, but she felt the voltage travel through her entire body.

Rex had seen the exchange, and he gave a low whistle when Violet rejoined him at the back of the room after her remarks.

"You weren't kidding about those two. I thought we had heat back in the day, but if they're coming to dinner, you might want to make sure there's a fire extinguisher handy." He chuckled.

Violet grinned. "No way. This fire is just getting started, and I have a feeling it might be built to last."

Finn was as nervous as a long-tailed cat in a room full of rockers. He didn't know what he'd gotten himself into. All these thoughts of love and romance had him out of whack, and now he found himself standing on her porch, clutching a fistful of bluebells, afraid to ring the damned bell.

He was a seventy-two-year-old man, for Pete's sake. He had no business asking this woman out on a date. She was way out of his league.

Of course they'd been good friends for as long as he could remember, but that didn't mean she'd be interested in going to dinner with an old farmer on her arm tonight. He was just about to turn and walk away when the door opened behind him.

"Are you going to stand there all day talking to yourself, or are you going to come in and ask me to dinner?"

Finn slowly turned around, his eyes meeting hers in surprise. She held two iced teas, offering one to him as she stepped aside so he could enter.

Susan Eden was a remarkable woman. They'd known each other since they were both newly married. She'd shown him great kindness when he'd lost Margaret and their infant daughter. He'd never forgotten that. He'd watched her raise Claire, and he was there in turn as her friend while she grieved. They'd been in the fabric of each other's lives for decades now.

Susan came down to the garden all the time, asking him advice on her own private beds. Her house was on the property too, near the horse barn, where she could watch her beloved animals in the pastures below. She'd lived a quiet life alone there since her divorce but had remained lightly involved in the day-to-day operations of the farm.

Finn would be a fool not to take his own damned advice. It was time to notice what had been right in front of him all along.

He smiled nervously, and forty years after they'd first met, he finally asked Susan out on a date.

CHAPTER
EIGHTEEN

India took extra care getting ready that night. She'd braided the front two pieces of her hair and pinned them back, leaving the rest of it down in loose waves. Her dress was a midnight-blue vintage Halston with a low-cut back that glided over body like liquid, making her feel particularly sexy. She wondered if it were really because of the dress or if it were because of how she knew Wyatt would react when he saw her in it. The thought made her stomach flutter.

India was glad to be having dinner with Wyatt's friends, but the thought of spending quality time with his mother-in-law definitely put her on edge. She hoped it wouldn't be awkward for Susan to see Wyatt with someone other than Claire. Wyatt had told her that Susan wanted him to be happy, but wanting it and seeing it right in front of you were two different things. India resolved to make sure she spent enough time chatting with Susan to put her at ease.

What was she even thinking? Put Susan at ease? How was meeting a woman who was only a guest for the week going to be a consolation for anyone who loved Wyatt? She was surprised when she thought about how welcoming Violet had been to her so far, and she wondered why Wyatt's friend wasn't being more protective of him.

Her mind was running wild now, and India could feel her nerves starting to fray, so she went in search of the bourbon, glad to be in possession of the entire bottle. She'd just taken a sip, feeling the amber liquid warming her insides, when she heard his footsteps on the gravel walk.

She turned in time to see him at the door, a new bunch of wildflowers in his hand.

Any previous thoughts she'd had about slowing things down went right out the window. She'd never seen a man cut such a dashing figure in a suit. His was dark blue and beautifully tailored, with a crisp light-blue shirt underneath. Instead of wearing a tie, he'd left the top button undone, framing his lightly whiskered face to perfection. The sun was lighting him from behind, making him look ethereal.

So, apparently, getting weak in the knees was really a thing.

How had this remarkable person remained alone for so long? She couldn't believe her good fortune in finding someone so authentic. His vulnerability was a huge turn-on, but it also terrified her. She didn't want him to ever feel hurt again, of that she was sure. He was a good man, a kind man, and she already felt conflicted at the thought of leaving him at the end of the week. Of what that might do to him. Of what it would do to her.

Leaving him was the furthest thing from her mind in that moment, though, as she moved toward the door.

Wyatt watched her move and found himself once again at a loss for words. She stirred up something unfamiliar, something he couldn't put his finger on. It was more than a physical attraction. He wanted her to feel like the stunning, capable, complicated, confident woman she was. There was satisfaction in seeing her realize all of those things about herself.

It clicked. With Claire, he'd been a caretaker; with India, he'd met an equal.

He offered her the bluebells.

"They're so lovely, but, Wyatt, you don't have to bring me flowers every night," India said, holding the door so he could come inside.

He looked her up and down appreciatively, shaking his head.

"I know I don't have to. I *want* to. But the way you look, it seems a little unfair to the flowers. They definitely don't measure up."

He was frozen there, just inside the doorway.

"That's some dress."

He made a conscious effort not to move any closer to her so he wouldn't be tempted to cancel dinner altogether.

"Thanks. Violet mentioned this was a special dinner, so I'm glad I threw this dress on at the last minute."

"Me too," he told her, smiling.

She could drink milk out of that dimple.

She took another sip of the bourbon to steady herself, then handed him the glass.

"You look pretty great yourself."

But *great* didn't begin to describe it. He was eye candy.

India carried the flowers to the sink and placed them in a tall glass with water, then set the arrangement next to her bed.

She was well aware of what he would see when she turned her back to him, but she couldn't know how great the effect actually was. Her hair filled in almost all of the void left by the dress, but there was a small exposed place on her back that made Wyatt reconsider his gallantry. He took a long drag of her drink.

India grabbed her clutch off the dresser and headed toward the door he held open for her. She felt his fingers brush almost imperceptibly at the small of her back as she passed through. The quickening was instantaneous, and she whirled around to meet him eye to eye on the threshold.

His eyebrow was cocked in mock innocence as he took a leisurely sip of her drink. She stared at him.

"Do that again, and we are going to be more than a little late," she warned him.

Her voice had been barely above a whisper, their faces only inches apart.

She studied him for a moment, then she leaned in to kiss him, but instead took his bottom lip between her teeth and bit gently before letting go. His face registered shock. His body told the rest of the story.

"Two can play that game, Wyatt. Now let's go to dinner."

India gave him a pointed look over her shoulder and headed down the walk. Setting the drink down, he followed her outside and shut the door behind him. He didn't take his eyes off her for a second.

Dinner in the barn was a special experience enjoyed by most guests who visited Blackberry Farm, but a meal in the wine cellar was both exceptional and exclusive. The table was set for twenty-four, resplendent with tall crystal vases brimming with forsythia, and enough candles of different shapes and sizes to give the room a dreamy glow. Each place setting held four stemmed wine glasses, prepared to receive the perfect pairing for each course.

Wyatt and India were one of the last couples to arrive, so they plucked two glasses of champagne from a passing tray and stepped outside onto the patio where guests had gathered for cocktails. It was a perfect evening, warm with little humidity, the moon just starting to peek up over the foothills.

Violet and Rex were standing off to one side, waiting for them to arrive. The women greeted each other with a hug while Wyatt and Rex exchanged a warm handshake. They chatted together for a few minutes about that day's class before steering the conversation to the special dinner. Violet was excited to share such a rare experience with them.

"The guest chef has an amazing reputation for using clean ingredients, so I'm excited to see what she'll come up with tonight. It should be incredible, considering the variety of foods she has to work with here. I read somewhere that she's eliminated the use of pasta altogether and only uses spiralized vegetables now. At least that part of the meal will be good for the waistline, even if the half-dozen glasses of wine won't. I guess tonight we'll play for the tie."

Violet offered her flute up in a toast before nudging Rex with her hip.

"Rumor has it she's gorgeous too: a Chinese father and an Italian mother. I've warned Rex to be on his best behavior or he'll be sleeping out in the hammock tonight."

The foursome chuckled together, sampling the mint-pesto mini bruschetta being passed by the servers. India was admiring the view over the valley, the fields dotted with East Friesian sheep that seemed to glow in the dusky light, when she heard Wyatt's surprised voice.

"I don't believe it. You old fox."

India spun around in time to see him staring open-mouthed at something across the patio. She followed his gaze and saw Susan Eden being escorted into the party by Finn, a scene that was causing quiet murmurs throughout the crowd. Finn was looking around nervously, nodding to familiar faces, but Susan looked completely at ease—ecstatic, really. She was even lovelier than India had remembered, perhaps in part because of her evident happiness. These were two people on a date; there was no mistaking that.

India watched Wyatt as he took it all in. His face was a blend of surprise and amazement, causing her to wonder if this was a new relationship, or at least new to him. She supposed it must be, or Wyatt surely would have mentioned it to her. Violet and Rex appeared to be thrilled by the turn of events, Violet rushing over to greet the couple with hugs, and Rex slapping the farmer on the back kindly.

"I take it you didn't see this coming," India said.

Wyatt finished the last sip of his champagne, then set his empty glass on a passing tray and swiped a new glass for each of them in the process.

"I can't say I did," he said. "If I didn't know better, I'd say Finn is upping the ante on me." Wyatt went to work on his second drink.

India watched him. He seemed unsettled for the first time since she'd known him. She didn't think it was the coupling of his loved ones that had him rattled; it seemed like something else.

"Upping the ante how?" she asked.

Wyatt looked at India with a curious expression on his face. She could tell he was carefully weighing his thoughts before he verbalized them.

"It's OK, never mind," she said, touching his arm, freeing him from feeling the need to explain. He shook his head, wanting to finish.

"When Finn and I talked the other day, he told me that I needed to be open to possibilities when they come my way. He worries that if I don't open up, there's no telling what might pass me by. He's afraid I'll end up alone like him."

He watched the older couple interact with each other, both of them clearly smitten. He still couldn't get over it.

"Although I guess he isn't alone now, is he? I suppose Finn decided to follow his own advice, thinking it might force my hand to do the same with you."

Wyatt looked back at her, waiting for his words to sink in, trying to gauge her response.

India felt the blush creeping up from her neck. So they'd discussed her. That alone didn't surprise her much, but learning about the depth of the conversation was unnerving. They'd obviously talked about the same things she'd been wondering herself. What was this? Whatever it was between them had grown legs and was suddenly feeling a lot less like a fling and more like a choice that would have to be made. She drained the rest of her champagne, grateful he'd thought to grab them each a second glass. Between that and the bourbon, she could feel her nerves starting to relax. She took a deep breath.

"Personally, I'd say you're doing a pretty good job of taking advantage of opportunities so far."

It was hard not to laugh at the shock on his face, so she did, and after a moment, he joined her. They finished their champagne, setting the empty glasses on a nearby table.

"Touché. If Finn only knew how much ground he has to cover to catch up . . . that would set the old man's bow tie spinning for sure."

Wyatt offered India his arm. It was beginning to get dark, so most of the guests, including their friends, had moved inside to find their seats for dinner.

Just before they reached the French doors leading inside, Wyatt stopped them short, pulling India into the shadows and tightly up against him. One hand rested on the small of her back, the other slipped under her hair, tilting her neck toward his face. He grazed her with his teeth, trading bites for kisses until she'd almost forgotten why they'd come tonight. As suddenly as he'd started, he released her, his fingers trailing down her backside and off the silken curve of her bottom. He clasped her hand and led her back toward the door.

"I want you to know that the message was received," Wyatt said.

They locked eyes. Wyatt squeezed her hand.

"I won't be missing a single opportunity from here on out."

They walked inside, hand in hand, to join the rest of the group for dinner.

CHAPTER
NINETEEN

India needn't have worried about the opportunity to make a connection with Susan. The women were seated next to each other at dinner, with Finn and Wyatt just across the table. Violet and Rex were at the other end of the long table, entertaining some guests of the visiting chef.

Susan was easy to talk to, sharing with India much of what she enjoyed about being the proprietress of Blackberry for all these years. She was interested in India's life in New York, and if she were privy to any of India's personal backstory, she was either too gracious or too discreet to mention it. They chatted easily about travel, current events, and other common interests.

"So what do you think of Blackberry Farm? Violet told me you've wanted to visit for a while. Is it what you expected?" Susan loved to hear feedback from guests, always looking for even the smallest thing they could improve upon.

India raised her glass in salute. "It's the most captivating place I've ever been. Really. It's remarkable what you've done here, creating such a luxurious experience but also a chance for people to truly get away from it all and relax. Every single person who works here loves their job, and it shows. I can't imagine leaving at the end of the week."

Susan was intrigued by this young woman who had captivated Wyatt. She was beautiful, smart, and confident, but Susan knew those superficial qualities wouldn't have been enough to change Wyatt so completely the way India had somehow managed to do. She also knew that India had a full life of her own back in New York, and she was well aware of the girl's recent adventures, thanks to a quick Google search. She respected her even more for taking a stand the way she had. If only Susan herself had said no instead of yes to the wrong man all those years ago.

But then she wouldn't have had Claire.

Whatever the case, the light was back on in Wyatt, and Susan felt her eyes sting with tears as she watched him talking animatedly with Finn across the table.

She was grateful for the chance to see him happy again. There were many times she'd wondered if it were even possible. She knew he'd always felt an irrational sense of loyalty to Claire's memory, and she wondered if she'd been wrong all those years ago to give them her blessing when everyone knew there was so little time left for Claire and even less hope. Watching him stay true to her daughter's memory over the years had both comforted her and made her feel guilty. She would love nothing more than to see this man she considered her son in love once again. She suspected she was witnessing the beginning of that now.

And Finn. She'd thought he'd never ask. They'd always shared a special connection over the years, even back when she was still married. Sharing the experience of a loss that painful with another human being will bond you for life. She'd thought Finn would die from the grief of losing his wife and daughter and was touched that he'd allowed her to be a friend to him during those dark days.

He'd been a rock for her too, when she lost her own sweet girl. But this thing between them had happened long before that. Watching him step up and be a father and a friend to Wyatt had been what had convinced her that she'd been in love with this man for a long time.

She couldn't believe she'd waited so long for him to realize the same thing, but now he'd finally come around. She supposed that seeing Wyatt happy had been the kick in the pants Finn had needed. She wasn't letting him get away now. She'd love him completely for whatever time they had left.

Finn looked across the table at Susan, and it was like everyone else in the room just faded into the background when she smiled back at him. He'd been such a horse's ass to drag his heels with her all these years. If he'd only known that she'd felt the same way, he would've made his move long ago.

She'd told him as much when she'd agreed to be his date for the night, and she'd surprised the hell out of him when she'd pulled him in for a kiss. He didn't know it could feel like this at his age, and man, oh man, he was sure excited to see if there were any more surprises in store. Their eyes twinkled at each other, and he reached his hand across the table to give hers a gentle squeeze.

"Laying it on pretty thick, aren't you?" Wyatt said. "I got the message, loud and clear."

Finn harrumphed, winking at Susan before letting her hand go.

"Just trying to show you how it's done, boy. Although, from the looks of things, you seem to have finally gotten your head straight all by yourself."

Finn smiled at Wyatt. "I'm happy for you, son. Really. She's a keeper."

Wyatt knew that she was, but he just didn't know how he was going to go about convincing India to stay. Watching her talk with Susan, and seeing how the two women had clicked, made his heart swell. Maybe it was time for him to stop over-thinking things so much and let his emotions take the lead. He knew what he had to do, though, and it made him edgy.

He had to tell her how he felt, but he didn't want to scare her. It wasn't normal to have these feelings for someone so quickly, and he wondered if he was crazy to even consider speaking them out loud. What if he didn't, though, and he lost this chance at happiness with someone he knew was his match?

He could feel the desperation overtaking his rational mind as he watched her excuse herself to use the restroom. There was a bustle of activity tableside, so he waited a few moments until everyone was distracted and then excused himself as well.

He'd noticed out of the corner of his eye that Violet was trying to get his attention for some reason, but he ignored her for now. Wyatt had important business to attend to. He supposed that he might as well start the rest of his life right that minute.

India was just coming out of one of the single restrooms when he rounded the corner and took her hand, leading her back inside. He locked the door and turned to her, his face awash with vulnerability. She stared at him with her big round eyes, and any fear he had faded away in that instant.

"This is going to sound crazy, but I am finding it hard to breathe when I think about you leaving here. It's like I'm in some crazy free fall, and you're the oxygen mask I'm wearing, the only thing making it better."

He stepped closer to her, their faces just inches apart. He reached for her, laying his hands on her shoulders, searching her eyes while he spoke.

"Please tell me you feel this too. I tried so hard to resist you, but there's something bigger at work here, India. From the moment I saw you in the airport, it's like I had to know you. And when you look at me like you're looking at me now, it renders me defenseless. I'm a goner. If you can tell me that it's purely physical for you, I'll try to let that be enough. God knows that part has been incredible. But I don't believe that's all this is. I don't know if I can be this person I'm becoming without you."

Time passed as they looked at each other, but neither of them knew how much. They searched each other's eyes for the answers.

"Wyatt, I don't know how this happened, but I've fallen in love with you. It's not just physical for me. I told you I knew something was missing from my life, and I know now. It was you. I'm scared and I don't understand it . . . but I know. I just—"

He stopped her there, his mouth meeting hers halfway. They felt themselves fuse together in that moment, each of them knowing that there was no return from this. They'd leapt, and now there might be hell to pay. They held on to each other for dear life, afraid to float back to the surface too soon.

They finally parted unwillingly, and Wyatt took her hands in his.

"I'm in love with you too, India. You've changed something in me, and I feel alive again. I don't know where we go
from here, but I promise you, when we leave tonight, I'm
going to show you just how sure I am."

He kissed her again, letting his hand linger in hers for a
moment before finally letting go, leaving her to collect herself
before rejoining him.

She looked at her reflection in the mirror. She was
unrecognizable. The woman looking back at her now was
someone she'd never seen before. She was a woman in love.

Smiling, she turned and opened the door and stepped
into the hallway. She was about to turn the corner to walk
back into the dining room, when she heard a voice behind her.

"Hello, India. Small world."

She whirled around.

Jack was standing in the shadows, his cold eyes looking
her up and down.

"Looks like I'm not the only one who's moved on, but,
really? A bathroom? Seems a little beneath you."

India was dumbstruck. She couldn't wrap her brain
around a possible scenario in which Jack would be standing
in front of her.

"Who's the poor bastard you're stringing along this time?"
He intended his words to sting, and they hit the mark. India
flinched and tried to collect herself enough to speak.

"What are you doing here, Jack?" Her brain still couldn't
reconcile seeing him in front of her. She couldn't make herself
understand.

He smiled smugly. "That delicious meal we all just
enjoyed? My girlfriend prepared it for you. I finally found a
woman who understands the value of taking care of people
other than herself."

India didn't know what to say in response to his attack, and she felt the tears start to fall as she heard footsteps coming down the hall behind her.

It was Violet, and she was mortified.

"India . . . I had no idea. Please forgive me."

"Forgive you for what?"

Wyatt had followed Violet down the hall, stopping short at the sight of India in tears.

He looked up and saw Jack standing there. The self-satisfied look on the man's face told him all he needed to know. His hands clenched at his sides, and he moved to position himself between this man and India.

"Who the hell are you?"

CHAPTER
TWENTY

Wyatt had never been in a fight in his life, but seeing India standing there with tears rolling down her cheeks made him think his streak might be over. She looked devastated. It was hard to imagine what could have happened in his brief absence. It had only been a few minutes. Whatever it was, he was certain it had something to do with the egotistical asshole who was standing before him. He could feel the man's contempt for India as he threw his hands up in mock surrender.

"Whoa, take it easy, pal. I was only saying hello." Jack took a step backward, feigning submission.

Jack turned toward India, gesturing to her, his smile not reaching his eyes when he spoke.

"India and I know each other well, don't we, love?" His grin was salacious and his tone overly familiar.

It was his choice of words, though, that had Wyatt fantasizing about dropping him right there in the hallway and then spreading his teeth like fertilizer in the fields tomorrow. Whoever he was, India was visibly rattled but doing her best to collect herself. She wiped the tears from her cheeks but didn't look up at Wyatt.

Violet stepped in, touching Wyatt on the arm in an attempt to calm him down. She'd never seen him this provoked.

"Wyatt, this is Jack Sterling. He's a guest of our visiting chef, Laina Ming."

Violet could see her words register with Wyatt; he looked confused still, but his hands relaxed a little at his sides.

"He's also my ex-fiancé," India said in an unsteady voice.

The sounds of other guests enjoying their coffee and dessert floated down the hall, spoons against dinnerware breaking the silence as the four of them stood together awkwardly, seemingly at a loss for words.

Jack spoke first. "Well, I hate to cut this charming reunion short, but I was just headed into the men's room. Nice to see you, India. Violet, I'll see you back at the table."

He looked at Wyatt.

"I'm sorry we got off on the wrong foot."

Jack offered Wyatt his hand; Wyatt refused it. Jack smirked, shaking his head in disbelief.

"Well, I hope you're better at making second impressions. Enjoy your evening."

Jack turned and pushed his way into the restroom, locking the door behind him.

Wyatt turned to look at India, who had closed her eyes and looked to be in physical pain. He was in disbelief. How had she ever considered marrying that motherfucker? He couldn't have been more different from what Wyatt had imagined.

Violet broke the silence.

"It's my fault. I wouldn't have invited you guys tonight if I'd made the connection. I didn't realize that Chef Ming was dating your ex, India. I only realized who he was once dinner had started."

She turned to India, her expression confused.

"What the hell did you ever see in him? He is the most pompous asshole I've ever met, nothing like he seems on TV. And Chef Ming is so kind and charming. And you're so . . . I don't get it." Shaking her head in disbelief, she rushed on. "I tried to get your attention to warn you both, but I couldn't catch your eye without making a scene."

India opened her eyes and looked up at Wyatt, who was starting to pace now, running his hands through his hair in frustration.

India let out a ragged breath, her voice not sounding like her own. "No one could have seen this coming. I mean, I guess there was something a while back in the tabloids about him dating a celebrity chef, but what are the chances she would be the one cooking here this week? I can't believe this. I feel sick to my stomach."

She was visibly shaking, her arms wrapped around herself in an effort to stop. Wyatt quit pacing and turned to look at the two of them with a stony expression. He shrugged off his jacket and walked over to place it around India's shoulders. Her gaze stayed on the floor in front of her, but she mumbled her thanks.

"Violet, take India back to the table. Let Finn and Susan know I'll be along in a minute; tell them to excuse my rudeness, but there's something I have to do."

Wyatt shot Violet a look that told her the plan wasn't up for discussion.

"Wyatt, please. Let's go back together," India said, her voice pleading.

She looked so wounded standing there draped in his jacket, her blue eyes brimming with tears. He turned away, wishing he could vaporize Jack Sterling.

"Nothing good can come of this. He hates me, and he has every right to."

Wyatt had his back to them now but visibly stiffened at India's words. Violet knew he needed time.

"He'll be along in a minute, India. Let's get back before this gets any worse. We don't need to give anyone a reason to talk; people will be wondering where we are if we don't get back."

Violet put her arm around India and gently steered her back toward the dining room while Wyatt folded his arms in front of him, determined to wait.

He was feeling a conundrum of things, but mostly he was just pissed. He'd finally told India how he felt, but that moment was tainted now. He rolled up his sleeves while he waited, not sure what he would say but knowing that he couldn't remain silent.

The door to the restroom opened, and Wyatt watched as Jack strolled out, distracted by the phone in his hand. He was reading something and smiling, not a care in the world, before he looked up and noticed Wyatt standing there. He clicked a button and shut his phone off, dropping it into his pocket. Wyatt got clarity in an instant.

"You wanted your second impression. Well, here it is. Why don't we talk about what you might have said to India that made her so upset?"

Wyatt knew he needed to remain calm, but his jaw was clenched so tightly it made it hard for the rest of his body not to follow suit.

He did not like this man.

Jack shrugged his shoulders and leaned nonchalantly against the wall, exhibiting a self-assurance that bordered on cockiness.

"Listen, I'm sure you're a good guy. Violet said great things about you at dinner, and she's terrific, so I'll give you the benefit of the doubt. But you don't know who you're dealing with here. India is a man-eater. You might think she's into you, but you'd better be damn sure you don't get screwed. Sure, it's possible she's even convinced herself that this time it's different. Trust me, that woman doesn't know what she wants. Besides, no one will ever be more important to her than her job. Take it from me. When you make it as high up the food chain as India and I have, it's tough to be with people who don't understand what it means to be at the pinnacle. Success can be lonely, my friend. You should find someone more . . . well, more like you."

Wyatt felt his blood run cold. Who knew what this narcissist had said to make India so upset, but if this little speech was any indication, he knew it couldn't have been good. He used words as weapons, and he used them effectively. There was no reason to waste another minute of his life on this person.

"You're not my friend, and I'm not so great that I won't ask you to leave this dinner in front of a room full of people. I suggest you get in there, make your apologies, and excuse yourself for the evening. I want you off this farm by morning. And you're right. The meal was delicious. No doubt, your girlfriend is a very talented chef. Unfortunately, when it comes to judging people, there's no accounting for taste."

Wyatt stepped aside, indicating Jack should exit before him. He took the cue.

"I'll gladly leave. I have no desire to sit at a table with that woman for even a minute longer. Hell, if I'd known she would be here, I never would have come. I'm here for Laina. But I'm telling you, you're making a big mistake. When this week is up, she'll go back to Manhattan and her one true love, leaving you here in this simple little place. You'd better enjoy it while it lasts." Jack grinned at Wyatt before turning to go. "I'd say I'll see you in New York, but, yeah . . . that's probably not happening."

Jack buttoned his jacket and returned to the dining room.

When Wyatt returned to the table, he found that the dinner had concluded, and guests had started to say their good-byes. Scanning the room, he couldn't find India, but he saw Violet and Rex standing with Susan, deep in conversation. He strode over to them, looking as disturbed as he felt. They turned to him, concern on their faces.

Susan placed her hand on his arm.

"Oh, Wyatt, I'm so sorry. Violet's told us what happened. I knew something was wrong when India returned to the table, but I had no idea."

She tilted her head to catch his eye. He'd still been looking around the room for India.

"Finn is walking her back to Woodshed. We weren't sure how long you'd be, and it was obvious that she needed to excuse herself, but we didn't want her walking alone. Are you OK?"

Wyatt nodded and grabbed his jacket off the back of India's chair where she'd left it. Violet pulled him aside as he was turning to go.

"What are you going to do, Wyatt? Stop and give yourself time to think. Please don't let that man get in the way of what was happening with the two of you. I've never seen you this happy. Ever. Please promise me you'll forget he was even here?"

She grabbed him for a brief hug before pulling back to look at him once more, her hands on his arms.

"It's not always going to be easy, Wyatt. But she's worth fighting for. Don't let her doubt that. And don't you doubt it either."

Violet turned back to her husband, leaving Wyatt alone with his thoughts.

Thoughts that were now riddled with doubt.

CHAPTER
TWENTY-ONE

Finn wasn't sure anything he could say would make a difference to her. He'd caught the gist of what had happened before they'd left but was a little fuzzy on the details. He could tell that, whatever it was, India was rattled to the bone, and there was no way he was letting her walk back to her cottage on her own.

They strolled in silence for the first few minutes, the gravel drive crunching under their feet, providing just enough white noise to make the quiet seem comfortable. It wasn't a long walk, and as they grew closer and could see the lights of the cottage, India found her words.

"Thanks for bringing me back, Finn. When I told you I looked forward to spending some time with you, this wasn't exactly what I'd envisioned." She shot him a rueful glance.

He shook his head and chuckled. "Hey, when you're my age, you'll take what you can get," he said. "Although, I must say, I'm starting to feel like it's my lucky day, spending time with not one but two lovely ladies this evening."

India smiled. "That was a nice surprise for everyone, I think . . . you showing up with Susan. For Wyatt most of all. Although I'm betting he hasn't told you that yet. I'm really sorry I ruined the end of your date. I'm OK now. You should head back over to be with Susan."

They stopped short of the walkway leading up to the porch. Finn tucked his hands into his pockets and turned to look out over the gardens, which were glowing under the bright light of the moon. They could make out the shadows from the rows of tiny shoots dotting the ground.

"You know, I can't believe it took me as long as it did to ask her out. We've known each other darn near forty years now, and my stubborn rear end took every bit of that to work up the courage. I thought my work here was enough to sustain me, and it was for a lot of years. But, you know, I wish someone had told my thirty-two-year-old self that my seventy-two-year-old self would know better and not to waste so much darned time."

He sighed, turning back to India.

"Wyatt is a good man. He's my son, and I love him. But if I know him at all, I know that what happened back there scared the bejesus out of him. He'll be looking for a reason to pump the brakes now. I hope you'll talk him out of that. You two seem well suited, and I'd kick myself if I didn't caution you both against wasting precious time like I have. You won't get it back, you know."

They stood in silence for a moment before India reached over to give him a hug.

"He's the best man I've ever known, Finn. You did right by him, and I thank you. I promise you we'll figure this all out, one way or another. The last thing I'd ever want to do is hurt Wyatt. I . . . he means so much to me too."

She wiped her eyes, unaware that she'd even been crying.

"Now go on. Susan waited a long time for this date, and you should give her a proper ending. I'm betting you'll get more than a hug good night too."

She smiled and patted him on the arm, charmed that the old farmer had had the good grace to blush.

India was still sitting on the porch steps when the beam from a pair of headlights swung around and lit her up. She couldn't bring herself to go inside, where the memories of Wyatt seeped from every space. She could only see his outline as he climbed down out of the truck and walked toward her. She raised her arm in a meek wave before resting her chin back down on the heel of her hands.

It was obvious she'd been crying, her face pink and her lips swollen. He thought she'd never looked more beautiful as she did then, in that moment of vulnerability.

Wyatt walked over to where she sat and offered her his hand. She took it.

"Come with me back up to the ridge. I think we have some talking to do." He gently pulled her up toward him, bending his head to brush her lips against his in a gentle kiss. Holding her hand, he walked her to his truck, and they climbed in and headed back down the road together.

Violet and Rex were sitting on the back porch of the farmhouse discussing the evening when they saw Wyatt's truck pull in over at Woodshed. Reaching over to swipe the beer they were sharing out of her husband's hand, Violet breathed a sigh of relief when she saw them get into the truck together.

"Thank God," she muttered. "Put those two together, and there's at least a fighting chance they'll find their way to the other side of this mess."

Rex reached down to grab another beer bottle out of the bucket of ice next to them. He popped the top and took a swig as he watched the fireflies light up the lower meadow.

"You know, when that dude first sat down across from me at dinner, I thought he looked familiar. But then he started talking, and I totally lost interest in trying to figure out why. What a dick. I'm glad you put the pieces together. That's why I married you. You're the smart one."

He leaned over and kissed his wife.

Violet loved this man. He made her laugh every single day, and he was damned good-looking. He was also an excellent judge of character, so if Rex thought Jack was an idiot, then Jack was an idiot.

"I still can't picture India with him. At all. I mean, they're so different."

Violet paused, looking out into the inky night.

"Do you question it at all—that she could feel the way she does about Wyatt? He's the complete opposite of weather boy."

The beer was starting to loosen her up, and her feisty spirit was shining through. Rex loved when she got fired up. She had his attention now.

"I don't know. Maybe you're not giving our boy Wyatt enough credit. Maybe she mistook that guy's arrogance for confidence. Wyatt is a pretty confident guy in his own right. They're both successful, and neither one of them's ugly, although if you tell Wyatt I said he's good-looking, I'll deny it until the day I die."

Violet almost spit out her beer laughing.

"My point is, they're more alike than you might think. The main difference between them is that Wyatt's kind. That's why she's drawn to him. I don't get the feeling she's experienced much of that in her life."

Rex rocked back in his chair, taking another drag of his beer. When Violet didn't say anything, he glanced over to see what was wrong.

His wife was staring at him like she'd never seen him before.

"Well, look at you, Dr. Freud. Aren't you just an expert in human behavior and romance?" She stood up and reached for him, pulling him out of his chair.

"Whaddya say we grab a couple of those beers and head upstairs so you can teach me a few other things about the game of love?"

She laughed out loud when he couldn't move fast enough.

Finn made it back just in time to watch Susan saying good night to the last of the guests. He watched her from across the room, still in awe that such an elegant, sophisticated woman would choose a simple man like himself. She took his breath away, even now in the twilight of their lives, and he intended to make every moment they had left together matter.

Susan was thanking Chef Ming when he walked up and slipped his arm around her waist. "It must be all the travel he's been doing lately; he said he was just feeling a little under the weather," Finn heard Laina explaining to Susan. "He wanted me to apologize for ducking out without saying good-bye."

Susan smiled graciously, despite the fact that she was well aware of why Jack had left early. Chef Ming was a smart woman. It wouldn't take her long to catch on to the scoundrel she was dating.

"Well, send him our best. And, really, the meal was sublime. Please accept our invitation to come back anytime. It was a pleasure to have you cook for our guests."

The women shook hands and said good night.

Finn marveled at her diplomacy.

"You handled that perfectly. A lot better than I might have. I hope Wyatt follows your example."

Susan reached over and gave him a kiss. They were alone now in the dining room. It was a place they'd been together many times for special functions over the years, but it suddenly felt very different to them both. Finn reached down and clasped her hand, his fingers intertwining with hers.

"What do you say I walk you home, Susie? If I'm lucky, we'll still have time for a little necking on the porch swing."

He gave her another quick kiss and a toothy grin.

Susan started walking toward the door, pulling him along behind her.

"Actually, Mr. Janssen, I was hoping you'd packed a toothbrush."

CHAPTER
TWENTY-TWO

They were quiet on the ride up to the Airstream, but Wyatt couldn't help reaching over and grabbing India's hand once they'd backed out of the drive. Now, as he rubbed his thumb in circles on the inside of her palm, it was hard to think about anything except comforting her. He wished he could forget how sad she'd looked when he'd pulled up and saw her sitting on the porch. He had a feeling that image was seared into his brain, a benchmark low for years to come.

Wyatt knew the conversation wasn't going to be easy, and he'd considered letting them both have the night to process what had happened, but the idea of missing out on any time together had had him steering the truck toward her without realizing he'd made the conscious decision to do so.

He glanced over at India, but she was facing the window, so he could only see a bit of her reflection in the glass, thanks to the dashboard lights. Something was different. She looked defeated, the confidence that he'd noticed that first day dried up and gone. He was lucky he'd gotten out of that cellar without pummeling her ex and embarrassing them all. Jack might as well have physically attacked her, for all the damage he'd done. Wyatt hoped he could convince her to consider the source, but deep down, he knew something had changed for him too.

They pulled to a stop in front of the trailer, and he put the car in park, killing the headlights. It was dark, the moon and stars providing the only light. By the time he'd gotten out and walked around to her side, she'd already climbed out of the truck and was standing with her back to him, arms folded, and looking out into the woods. He put his arms around her and she leaned her head back into him. He could feel her crying quietly as she turned to bury her head in his chest. They held each other tightly until her tears began to subside.

"It kills me to see the power he has over you," Wyatt said. "It took everything in me not to punch him in his smug face. India, I don't know what he said to you, but you can't let him have this much control."

He was rubbing her back as she pulled away to look up at him.

"That's just it."

India sniffled and wiped her eyes with the backs of her hands.

"What he said was right. I'm terrified of what we're doing here. Wyatt, I meant what I told you tonight. I love you. I'm in love with you. So much that it scares me. But what are we doing? How can our lives possibly fit together to make this work? I'm so disgusted with myself for putting you in a position to get hurt again. I'll always regret that I've allowed myself to be so selfish. If you knew me, you'd know it's my dominant characteristic. All Jack did was remind me of that."

He pulled completely away from her, his eyes flashing with frustration.

"That's complete and total bullshit. In the time that I've known you, I haven't seen you be selfish even once. In fact, you've been anything but. My friends adore you, and Susan and Finn are ready to kick me out of this place and adopt you instead. These are quality people that feel this way about you, India. Why would you put so much stock in what that asshole thinks? You're better than that. You're stronger than that. I've seen it, and it's one of the things I love about you. One of the many things. I'm so in love with you, India, and if you think what happened tonight changes that, then you're crazy."

He watched her eyes as she took in his words. She was quiet and turned away from him again. He didn't want to push, so he took the opportunity to stack some wood and start a fire in the pit. He reached inside the trailer and grabbed a plaid fleece blanket off the couch and two beers from the fridge, and when he came back outside, she'd moved closer to the warmth of the blaze. Even though she'd put his jacket back on in the car, he'd felt her shivering when he held her, so he wrapped the blanket around her and moved away to sit in one of the chairs. She followed, sitting next to him.

India knew she owed him an explanation. This man she'd only met a week ago had turned her entire world upside down. She didn't know if it was this place, or their insane chemistry, or her own need. She couldn't be sure how she would feel once she got back to her life in New York. He deserved to know that about her. She took a deep breath.

"I've spent most of the last decade devoting all of my efforts to my career. Honestly, I knew I would from a very early age. I was determined not to get stuck at home like my mother had."

She swallowed hard, finding the strength to continue. Wyatt watched her, knowing better than to interrupt her with questions. He would let her set the pace.

"My mom spent most of my childhood in bed. She suffered from severe depression, and I guess motherhood made it worse. So she avoided me and I let her. My father left us when I was a newborn, so I took care of her and myself until I graduated high school and escaped to college. I never looked back."

She looked at him for the first time since they'd sat by the fire. It was clear she was struggling with what came next. He reached over and squeezed her hand, urging her to continue.

"My mother took her own life my junior year in college. I lived with the guilt of leaving her back in Iowa for a long time, but I know now, after lots of expensive therapy, that was her journey. She didn't have an easy time on this planet, and that had to do with her own childhood, not mine. That's when I really decided that I would build my own life around my career. It was a safe . . . a selfish choice."

Wyatt reached over and covered their clasped hands with his free hand. He'd lost his own parents, so he understood that aspect of her pain, but he couldn't imagine how utterly abandoned she must have felt having a parent who had committed suicide and another who'd chosen to leave. No wonder she was so intent on being self-sufficient.

He weighed his words carefully before speaking.

"God, India. I'm so sorry. You're such an incredible person, and to accomplish what you have in spite of it all . . . it makes you even more remarkable in my eyes."

He brought her hand to his lips for a kiss. He was humbled that she would share something so deeply personal with him. They were knee-deep in it now, so he felt comfortable asking her the question that puzzled him most.

"What was it about Jack that made you reconsider marriage?" He had to know what she'd seen in him.

India sighed, shaking her head as if to clear it.

"I've had some time now to think about that, and I can honestly say that I know it wasn't Jack I was saying yes to—it was the idea of not being alone anymore. More than that, though . . . I felt like, at thirty-three, I was supposed to say yes. I got caught up in the moment, and when my bosses were so enthusiastic about the publicity, it felt impossible to find a way out without feeling like my job security was being threatened. Also, Jack really isn't as bad as he seemed tonight. I think his ego is still pretty bruised, and that's where all the bravado comes from."

Wyatt sat back in his chair and threw his foot over one knee.

"He's lucky that's all that's bruised after the way he treated you tonight." He gave her a rueful smile. "You're lucky I'm a lover, not a fighter."

He reached down and popped the top on the beers he'd forgotten, handing one to India. They sat quietly for a moment, each lost in their own thoughts. He couldn't shake the other question that had been on his mind all night.

"I know your career is important to you, India . . . rightfully so. Violet tells me you're amazing at what you do. But is that enough? I guess . . . I mean . . . do you think it will be enough for you now?" Their eyes met, and the air felt very still as he waited for her to answer.

India hadn't realized she was holding her breath. She sighed and looked at him, her eyes full of sadness.

"I wish I knew the answer to that, Wyatt. I feel like the only way to know for sure is for me to leave here on Friday, and see how we both feel once we have some distance between us. You have a lot to process too, deciding to put down roots here for the next year. What if you hate it and decide to spend the rest of your life traveling? This is going to be a huge lifestyle change for you. It's been such a whirlwind of a week in so many ways. We need to make sure that one or both of us hasn't been swept up in a moment that we can't get out of. Does that make sense?"

She watched her words sink in, feeling a little sick at hearing herself being so pragmatic. What if she was wrong to give him space? What if she decided she couldn't live without him, while he realized he was better off on his own? She knew she couldn't risk hurting him by not being absolutely sure, so she held her tongue, despite the urge to tell him she couldn't imagine leaving him.

Wyatt stood up, pacing toward the other side of the fire. He stood for a moment, lost in thought. He knew he was at a crossroads here; he could feel that the weight of his reaction would determine everything going forward. He decided to do what he'd always done when faced with an impossible decision. He went with his gut.

He started speaking without turning to look at her.

"I hear what you're saying, and while it tears me up to think of you leaving, I understand why you think you have to."

He drew a ragged breath and turned around to face her, his face lit up by the roaring fire. She could see the raw emotion in his eyes from ten feet away.

"I'm willing to take that bet, India. I think what we have here is so powerful, so all-encompassing and larger than life, that I'm willing to let you go to get you back."

She felt herself gasp a little. His words touched her deeply, but it was what he asked her next that would change everything.

"I'll let you go under one condition."

He started walking toward her, a different look in his eye altogether. This one gave her goose bumps.

"You spend the next thirty-six hours letting me show you all the reasons to believe in us. Let me love you, India. Starting right now."

He reached for her hand, pulling her up out of the chair.

CHAPTER
TWENTY-THREE

Wyatt led India inside the Airstream, ducking back out to make sure the fire was sufficiently dying. India watched him through the window as she slid out of her heels, his back testing the limits of his dress shirt as he worked to cover the remaining embers. India glanced around and noticed an old radio on the sink top and walked over to switch it on. The grainy sound of a Dierks Bentley song came on, urging her to move a little closer, closer. She shivered in anticipation and turned around to look out at Wyatt, but he was already standing in the doorway behind her, his hands clasping either side of the frame, one foot propped on the top step, watching her.

Their eyes met, and Wyatt entered the trailer before she knew what was happening, closing the space between them. He held her face in his hands, brushing her cheek with his thumb.

"Do you know what you do to me?"

He heard her sigh, her eyes closing and then opening as she answered him.

"This isn't fair, Wyatt. You're not playing fair."

She moaned as he roughly tugged his jacket off her shoulders and let it fall to the floor. His lips found the side of her neck, their softness contrasting with the rasp of his stubble and making her insides turn to jelly.

"No one said anything about playing fair, India. I want you, and I'm taking what I want."

He was consuming her, the sensation of his mouth on her enough to make her surrender before the battle had even begun.

Her hands made quick work of the buttons on his shirt, tearing the last two open impatiently in a need to get her hands on him. His muscled torso was the definition of sexy, and she slid her hands down his arms as she peeled his shirt off before she could stop herself.

His hands were roaming now too, gliding up and down the silk of her dress, the flimsiest of barriers between them. He forgot himself when she began to undo his belt, sliding it out of his pants in one quick motion, the heavy buckle dropping to the floor with a thud. She stared at him with a challenge in her eyes.

He had her now. He reached for her again, but she stepped back, away from him.

Her eyes were smoldering as she turned around and gathered her loose hair up in her hands, giving him access to the drawstring of her dress.

"Undress me, Wyatt," she said, as if he needed any direction.

He stepped toward her and reached for the silky cord, pulling it slowly until it released, the dress skimming off her body and into a pool at her feet.

She stepped out of it, but instead of turning toward him, she glanced over her shoulder as she walked slowly toward his bed.

"Are you going to stand there all night, or were you going to try and convince me of something?"

Yep. He was definitely in over his head. If this was a dream, he never wanted to wake up.

He knew that Michelangelo, if given the choice, would have chosen to immortalized her over David any day. She was perfect, and he memorized every curve as she walked away from him.

He closed the gap between them in a hurry, grabbing her by the waist and spinning her around to face him. He took her hands in his, intertwining their fingers, pulling back to look at her once more.

"You are the most incredible woman I've ever met, India. I'm consumed by you, and I'm about to show you just how much."

He pulled her back to him, every inch of her against him now, and kissed her urgently.

India heard the warning bells but ignored them. Somehow, she knew that this was the point of no return, but if that were so, then she never wanted to go back. She deepened their kiss as she reached down between them, unbuttoning his pants and sliding them and his briefs down in one swift motion.

Wyatt stepped wildly out of both garments, the air between them electric now as they fought to maintain both the kiss and the ability to breathe at the same time. He gasped as she took him in her hand, pulled him up against her, and began to stroke.

She filled up his senses, and before he could stop himself, he'd pushed her toward the bed, both of them falling together in a tangle on top of the down comforter.

India could feel how much he wanted her, but her need to regain control took over.

She rolled him onto his back, pinning his hands above his head. He couldn't believe how beautiful she looked, her hair tangled and wild, the skin of her neck and shoulders pink from him. She gave him a half smile before tossing her hair to the side and scattering kisses down his torso, her fingers tracing a circle around him.

Wyatt was writhing around, trying his best to let her take the lead, but it was impossible. When her hair scattered across his chest, it was all he could take, and he pulled her back up to him. He rolled her over onto her back and poised himself just above her.

She could feel him there, ready to merge them together, but he stopped. Looking into her eyes, his face was as serious as she'd ever seen it.

"I'm so in love with you, India. I hope that, no matter what, you know that now and always."

She pulled him down into her then, the two of them lost in each other, but also found.

🍓

They had no idea what time it was, but the light outside had changed as the moon prepared to switch places with the sun. She got up and wrapped herself in the fleece blanket, padding over to the doorway to peek outside. Morning was breaking, and she could hear the birds announcing the start of another day.

Her last full day with him.

She was resting her head against the doorjamb, considering it all, when she heard the click.

She glanced over to where she'd left Wyatt in bed. He was awake now, his camera in his hand, pointed at her. She smiled shyly at him, reaching up instinctively to smooth her hair. He lowered the lens.

"I never want to forget how you look right now, in this light. I hope we can look at this photograph in forty years and tell our children that this is the moment their mother decided she couldn't live without me."

India walked back over to the bed, crawling in next to him. She laid her head on his chest as he wrapped them both in the comforter.

"You have my heart, Wyatt. I just need to make sure that I can fully give myself to you, and I won't know that until I get back to the life I've worked so hard to build. I'm not sure how important that life is anymore, and that terrifies me, especially since it's only been a week. I need some perspective, and I know you can't see it now, but you do too. You deserve someone who can give themselves to you completely. I don't know if I'm capable of that. Yet."

She propped her head up on her elbow and looked at him.

"I don't want to put a time frame on it. I think we'll both know when we know. But maybe for the first couple of weeks, we should try not to talk so we can get real clarity."

She saw his frown and placed her hand tenderly on his cheek.

"I know that if I hear your voice, I'm not going to be able to think clearly. We have to figure out if this can work for real, Wyatt. That will only come with time and space."

He rolled onto his back and sighed.

"I know you're right, India, and I hate that I seem so needy. I promise you I'm not that guy. It just sucks when you meet the person you want to call your family . . . and . . . I guess I just want to start building that life without wasting another minute."

He looked at her.

"I'm the man I want to be when I'm with you. But I understand that sometimes you have to tear something down first to build something better. I'm willing to bet on us."

She smiled, her eyes full of tears, and leaned over to kiss him.

"I love you, Wyatt Hinch. There's no mistaking that. Let me show you how much."

CHAPTER
TWENTY-FOUR

It was the final day of the workshop, and Wyatt was teaching, so he drove India back to Woodshed so she could change her clothes. On the ride, she glanced over and saw him clamp his hand down over his mouth, a poor attempt at hiding a huge grin.

He was so handsome. His curls were still damp from their shower, and he'd trimmed his whiskers a little closer, showing off his chiseled jawline. She could've stood there all day watching him shave, wearing only a white towel around his hips.

"What's so funny?" she asked.

She could tell he was trying hard not to laugh. He was perfection in a simple black T-shirt and jeans.

"I was just thinking that if we keep this up, I'd better get a sign to hang on the Airstream door, 'If the trailer's rockin', don't come knockin.'"

He stole a look at her and laughed even harder when he saw her jaw drop.

"What? I mean, it was about time I broke her in! I owe you one, really."

He was obviously pleased with his attempt at humor.

"You did not just say that! Wyatt!" She couldn't help it, cracking up in spite of herself.

It was so easy between them.

He'd made them both coffee before they'd left, thinking as he'd added creamer to hers that he could get used to doing that small kindness for her for the rest of his life. He prayed she'd give him the chance.

They were rounding the bend by the barn, just across from Susan's house, when he pulled the truck off the side of the road and threw it in park. Reaching into the backseat, he pulled out his camera bag and started to open it.

"C'mon. We have a minute," he said. "I want to photograph you on the bridge."

India looked at him like he was crazy. She was wearing her dress from last night, with Wyatt's blue shirt over it, tied in a knot to hide where she'd ripped his buttons. Her feet were bare, her shoes on the backseat.

"Oh, you want to capture my 'drive of shame' look?"

India rolled her eyes at him, convinced he was still teasing her.

Wyatt had taken his camera from the bag and removed the lens cap, but he stopped at her words. He turned his shoulders so he was facing her head-on.

"A photograph is about capturing a feeling, a moment in time. I want to remember this morning with you forever, India. Besides, you manage to look more beautiful every second I spend with you. Blackberry Farm agrees with you. Or maybe love does."

He reached over and gave her a tender kiss.

She sighed when he pulled away.

"Well, when you put it like that, how can I say no? I just hope nobody comes along and sees me barefoot and in my clothes from last night. Make it quick."

She flipped down the visor mirror to take quick stock of her face, which was completely devoid of makeup. She pinched her cheeks and borrowed a swipe of his ChapStick from the cup holder, running her fingers quickly through her knotted hair. Wyatt had come around to her side and opened her door, and as she stepped onto the running board to get down, he scooped her up in his arms.

"Allow me. I don't want you to step on anything sharp."

He carried her the few yards to the bridge, setting her gently down on the weathered boards, but not before kissing her once more, deeply this time.

The sun was just cresting in the meadow behind the bridge, lighting India up from behind. Wyatt backed up a few feet and looked at her through his lens.

She was exquisite. Her hair told the story of their time together in bed, the golden light of the sun illuminating it like a halo around her head and shoulders. He could just make out her expression, the love in her eyes. His heart skipped a beat. She was his muse, and he would never have another. As he snapped the picture, he knew it would be magnificent but that it could never tell the whole story as perfectly as this moment did.

He walked back over to her, scooping her up again, and carried her back to the truck.

"Promise me that when you're back in New York, you'll find a place to get quiet and hear the answer, India."

She looked up at him, not certain what he meant.

"I just mean . . . when you're figuring out what you want. You'll have to be quiet to hear the answer. I can hear it now, when I'm with you."

He held her gaze.

"Love is the answer," he said.

🍓

Susan had gone out to the garden to cut some fresh mint for her morning tea when she saw Wyatt's truck pull off by the bridge. She watched the two of them, Wyatt photographing India, the love between them evident. Susan felt like a voyeur.

She hadn't realized that she'd been standing there with her hand over her heart until she heard the screen door slam, and looked back to see Finn coming down the steps in his overalls.

"Good morning, Susie. What's got you out here rooting around so early?"

He looked across the drive to where Wyatt was carrying India back to the truck, smiled, and reached down to grab Susan's hand.

"I never thought I'd live to see it, Sue. He's finally opened up, after all this time. Hell of a woman there, to finally get through to the ornery cuss."

He looked over at her as it dawned on him that she might have mixed emotions.

"Is it hard for you to see him with someone else?"

Susan sighed, shaking her head and smiling sadly.

"You know, I wondered if it would be, but strangely, it's comforting to see him so happy. It feels like his love for Claire wasn't the ruin of him after all, and I'm glad of that. I've lived with the guilt of encouraging them to marry when I knew there was no hope for years. It feels like that spell is finally broken. India is an incredible, accomplished woman, and I think she's a great partner for him."

Finn nodded in agreement.

"She's a perfect match for him, if you ask me," he said.

Susan raised her eyebrows and tilted her head, a question on her face.

"I'm just worried that she won't realize that what they're experiencing is so rare, that her job will be too much to walk away from. She has a big life in New York. What if she's leaving here before they've really had enough time to solidify what they've started? I worry that Wyatt won't bounce back from a broken heart this time. I wish there were a way to convince her to stay longer, let this love take root."

She reached down to pick up her basket of herbs, placing the mint on top and gathering her garden gloves and shears.

"Look how long it took us, for Pete's sake! We wasted decades, when we both just wanted to be together. What a couple of mules."

Her steely blue eyes looked up into his.

"I'm not wasting another day, Finn Janssen. I know I'm not the young woman that you had a crush on all those years ago, but if last night is any indication, we still have a few good years ahead. Why don't we show those kids by example? When you know, you know, right?"

She set the basket back down, grabbing both of his hands in hers. She could stare up at his handsome, suntanned face all day long, particularly when the lines of his eyes were crinkled up in a smile like they were now.

"I know this is crazy, but why should we waste another minute? This farm—this common ground we stand on—it's a place we created together, Finn. I want to grow old here with you."

He raised a brow at her. She smiled.

"OK, older, then. I want to live with you here in this place we've made. And I want to do it as your wife. What do you say? Will you marry me, Finn? And will you do it tonight, after dinner, surrounded by our guests? What better way to make them feel at home?"

He smiled at this woman who'd been a partner and friend to him for so many years. Be damned if she couldn't still surprise him. He took his hat off and rubbed his head, looking at her incredulously.

"Susie, nothing would make me happier than to wake up as your husband for the rest of my days. And, as for tonight, it just so happens I'm free. What exactly did you have in mind?"

"I'll fill you in on the details once we've consummated this engagement."

She stood on her tiptoes, reaching up to give her fiancé a kiss.

CHAPTER
TWENTY-FIVE

Jack Sterling could count on a solid five hundred retweets on any given day. He'd created quite a following for himself on social media after his life-and-death tweet from the plane and his subsequent failed attempt at marriage. He'd managed to parlay the drama into his own little cottage industry, and his fans were insatiable.

That morning, when he'd retweeted the article he'd anonymously fabricated for Page Six, he'd rocketed up over twelve thousand retweets. Apparently, the public was still hungry for details about "Jindia," and he'd been happy to provide them.

India got the news when she answered her phone and heard Julia's breathless voice on the line. She'd been just about to walk out the door to head to her final landscape workshop when the vibrating phone got her attention. She unplugged it from the charger and answered as she walked out the door. Julia barely gave her time to say hello.

"That son of a bitch! I can't believe he would stoop so low. I mean, of course he would, but seriously! What are you going to do? I think you should send out a counter tweet immediately! I mean . . . who would believe that you would be stalking him? Except Internet trolls, of course. Twelve thousand retweets? Yuck."

India tried to make sense of what Julia was saying, but she couldn't get a word in. She was sitting in her golf cart now, too stunned to start driving.

"Jules . . . slow down. What about Jack and Twitter? What are you talking about . . . stalking?"

She couldn't believe Jack would have mentioned anything to anyone about last night. He'd been asked to leave! Why would he make that public?

"You mean you don't know? Oh God, India. He insinuated that you were stalking him! Well, actually he retweeted an article that quoted an anonymous source that claims you followed him and his girlfriend—that chef—to their resort in Tennessee, and that you cornered him at dinner, begging him to take you back. Why would he retweet a story like that unless he'd planted it? It's total fiction! And how the hell does he know where you are? He's the stalker! You have to set the record straight."

India couldn't believe it. Jack was a master at making her look like a fool. His forlorn photo shoot after she'd dumped him, and now this? This kind of thing could permanently ruin her reputation, even if she came out and denied it immediately. A retweet wasn't the answer. Especially since, technically, it wasn't total fiction, and it was her word against his.

"Jules . . . of course it's a lie. I mean . . . mostly. Jack was here last night, and I did run into him at a private dinner that we both attended. His girlfriend was the guest chef, but her visit was planned ages ago. The rest is a crock. Wyatt actually kicked Jack out after he made an ass of himself. No one knows it, though, because it was just the two of them in a hallway, and Wyatt generously allowed him to save face by saying he was sick. Oh God, why would he do this?"

"Because he's an asshole, India! How are you going to handle it? You can't let people think he's telling the truth when they find out you actually were there at the same time. What do you think your bosses will say? You need to hang up right now and call the network. Make sure you let them know your side of the story. You can't let him win."

India knew Julia was right. She had to get out in front of this, and she knew calling Jack and begging him to deny the story was hopeless.

"Thanks, Jules. I'll call you tomorrow when I'm back in New York. I'll do what I can to make this right. Love you, friend."

India hung up and scrolled through her contacts. Finding her general manager, she dialed the number and spent the better part of the next half hour doing her best to clean up Jack's mess.

🍓

Workshop guests spent that final day photographing several different locations around Blackberry Farm, enjoying one-on-one time with the instructors. The entire group started on a hill overlooking the boathouse near the main guesthouse, with plans to fan out in three different directions on the property. The final dinner that evening would once again be held in the Yallerhammer Pavilion.

Wyatt was surprised not to see India when it came time to split into groups, especially since he'd dropped her off over two hours before. He waited as long as he could for her to show up before finally taking his guests and heading off toward the stables.

Rex was taking his group over to the dairy, and Violet was just about to head over to where they raised the Lagotto Romagnolo truffle puppies, when India pulled up in her golf cart, clearly flustered.

Violet motioned for her to join her in her own cart while the other guests followed behind.

Violet waited until they had some distance from the group.

"You really dodged a bullet with that guy. He's the stalker. What a world-class asshole."

India's head snapped up, realizing that, somehow, Violet already knew what had happened. She couldn't imagine how she'd heard. The woman certainly kept her ear to the ground.

Violet looked chagrined.

"This is the part where I admit to following you and Jack on Twitter back when you were engaged."

She couldn't bring herself to make eye contact with India, biting her lip in embarrassment.

"I'd forgotten all about it until this morning. I usually ignore notifications from social media, but when my phone blew up with retweets . . . well, it was hard to miss. I can't believe he would do that to you."

She steered the cart down the hill, past fields full of horses and sheep.

India shook her head, determined to move on. Fortunately, her station had believed her, suggesting that they had a way to make sure the public knew exactly what she'd been doing in Tennessee—and it wasn't stalking the competition's meteorologist. It was in the network's best interest to squash that notion.

NBC would issue a press release stating that India was on assignment for the network, in preparation for an upcoming piece on Blackberry Farm and heirloom farming. It was a win for her and a win for the resort. She was relieved to have gotten out of the whole mess relatively unscathed.

"I've tried to give Jack the benefit of the doubt, but he won't get sympathy from me after this stunt," India said. "I know he was hurt when I called things off, but I protected his reputation the best I could. It's clear he's never had the same concern for mine."

She waved her hand dismissively.

"The network is going to make it right, thank God. They are going to say I was here for a story, which will hopefully benefit the farm too. So all's well. I'm not letting this ruin my last day with"—she caught herself—"at Blackberry."

Violet looked at her and smiled.

"I'm glad to hear that. I know a certain teacher who was pretty bummed his favorite student was tardy this morning. Why don't I swing by the stables and drop you off? I'm sure he has a few last things he'd love to teach you."

They laughed together as Violet swung the cart into a last-minute U-turn.

Wyatt saw the two of them flying down the cart path toward him, Violet's red hair and India's blonde fanned out behind them. They were laughing together as they pulled up, a sight he hoped he'd get to see more of.

She fit him. His friends, his family. His life. He hoped she would come to the same conclusion when she went back to New York, but the alternative scared the shit out of him. He shook the thought away, determined to make the most of this last day and night with her. Then it was up to fate. And India.

They spent the next several hours looking at the world differently, experiencing the beauty of East Tennessee through the lens. India loved listening to him talk with the other guests about his passion, and found her own love for the genre reignite. She'd forgotten what a rush it was to capture an image at the exact moment when the light was perfect.

The sheep's woolen white faces and pink ears in the leafy green meadows where they grazed, late-afternoon sun casting shadows in all the right places.

Perfection.

She could hardly wait to edit and print the photos she'd taken. She felt so connected and satiated, and it was supremely satisfying on so many levels. She'd found the sweet spot. It had been a long time coming.

The guests said good-bye to each other, promising to reunite in an hour for drinks and dinner. India hung back, waiting for the last couple to thank Wyatt before they drove away. He slung his camera strap over his shoulder and turned to walk toward where she stood on the bank of the river.

She loved this man. She knew it in her bones now.

India raised her camera and snapped a quick series of him as he approached. His face changed from happy to surprised and, as he got closer, to something else altogether. She lowered her camera, throwing it over her shoulder as he reached for her, drawing her into his embrace. They stood there, holding each other, listening to the river hurry by them.

Everything else was insignificant. She felt intoxicated when he swept her hair behind her ear to whisper, "I want to make out with you so badly right now, but I've promised myself I'm going to wait until after dinner. But you should be ready after that. Really ready."

He pulled back to look at her, his dimpled smile teasing, but not. She couldn't help but laugh, shivering in anticipation. She'd be ready.

They turned to walk toward Woodshed, their hands clasped, excitedly talking about their day behind the lens the whole way back.

CHAPTER
TWENTY-SIX

Dinner was a festive affair, with everyone in great spirits, passionately discussing what they'd learned that week. They'd gotten to know each other well and promised to keep in touch, some even vowing to return to take the workshop again the following year. Jeff invited them all to visit his shop in Austin, and India had to admit that she'd even grown to like Annabelle and Virginia, despite the fact that they'd never given up on Wyatt. By the end of the week, though, she wondered if that wasn't just part of their shtick. They were funny, and they clearly loved each other. She found herself wishing she'd been able to have that kind of experience with her own mother, however flawed she'd been.

The farewell dinner was incredible. There were dozens of linen-clad tables set with lovely crystal and gorgeous spring flowers. India and Wyatt sat with Finn, Susan, Violet, and Rex, the six of them having great conversations and lots of laughs.

She loved his friends and family and knew it would be almost as hard to leave them as it would be to leave Wyatt.

Almost.

The meal had just wrapped up with an incredible chocolate soufflé when Susan tapped Wyatt on the shoulder, pulling him aside for a private moment. Finn stood with them, and India could see that whatever they were discussing had weight to it. Wyatt's face grew serious as he listened to each of them speak. She could tell that whatever they were saying, it was a surprise to him. He ran his fingers through his hair like she'd noticed he always did when he was caught off guard. When they'd finished talking, Wyatt reached out to hug them, first Susan, then Finn. India looked away, not wanting to intrude on such a personal moment.

Beyond the pavilion, out on the lawn, she could see that a large number of the staff had gathered, each of them holding a candle. She was wondering whether this was some kind of Blackberry Farm tradition, when she felt Wyatt return to her side and take his seat. He reached over, forgetting where they were, and kissed her tenderly. India could feel eyes on them, but she didn't care. She laid her palm against his face.

"Is everything OK? I saw you talking to Susan and Finn." She didn't want to overstep, but it was clear that something was on his mind.

"Yes. Great, actually." He smiled that easy smile, but it was obvious there was something he wasn't saying.

Just then, Violet tapped her glass to get everyone's attention.

"Rex and I would like to thank you all so much for a wonderful week. We hope you've enjoyed yourselves and that you've been able to relax in this beautiful place."

Everyone nodded in agreement, grateful for the time they'd all spent together. Violet smiled.

"We hope you've learned something about photography that you'll take with you and share, and we'd be honored if you'd join us again for another workshop sometime."

She paused, grabbing Rex's hand and motioning for Wyatt to join them. He stood and walked over to them.

"If you do decide to come back between now and this time next year, you'll be in the very best hands. Wyatt has agreed to stay on as the resident photographer here at Blackberry Farm while my husband and daughter and I spend a year working abroad. Wyatt'll be doing all of the teaching, along with shooting the promotional materials. We hope he's not too good, though, or we won't have jobs to come back to!"

They all laughed together before applauding the news. Wyatt raised his glass to the crowd. "A toast: To Violet and Rex, safe travels. To a great group of people and an incredible week, and hopefully, many more to come." He looked directly at India. "And . . . to love. Cheers."

Glasses clinked, toasting new friendships formed and lessons learned.

Wyatt took a big sip of his beer, smiled at India, and then continued. "We told you at the beginning of the week that we always want our guests to feel like family when they're here."

He looked over at Finn and Susan and nodded to them.

"So much so, we have a special treat for you tonight."

India saw Susan and Finn get up and start to leave the pavilion, walking out among the employees that had gathered in the yard. They joined another person who was standing on the pond's dock, which had been lined with tea lights. India looked back at Wyatt, who had also seen them leave and was now grinning from ear to ear.

"Ladies and gentleman, we would like to request the honor of your presence as we witness the marriage of two very special people. Please join me, along with the rest of the staff of

Blackberry Farm, who've gathered here tonight, to attend the wedding of Susan Eden and Finn Janssen."

The crowd gasped, then spontaneously erupted into cheers and applause. Everyone moved out into the yard, lit up by the flickering candles, and gathered as close to the dock as possible. As she neared the pond, India could see that a minister was waiting for them there. Finn and Susan were holding hands, looking very much in love.

Wyatt walked up beside India, slipping his hand into hers. She turned to look at him, the tears in his eyes barely visible in the darkness. She slipped her arm around his waist, and they watched together in awe as the two people who'd loved Wyatt the most promised themselves to each other for eternity.

The wedding was short but poignant, the groom joking that they'd wasted so much time, they needed to hurry up and get on with the honeymoon. Guests and staff would talk about sharing that special evening with them for years to come.

India and Wyatt said good night and then strolled together back to her cottage, each of them desperately aware of the ticking clock. Her flight was leaving Knoxville just before noon the next day, and Wyatt had promised to take her to the airport after breakfast. Neither of them wanted to think about that now.

Instead, they talked about what a lovely surprise it was to have the entire staff on hand for the wedding ceremony, and how it was so like Susan and Finn to want them there. Wyatt was happy but still a little stunned.

"I can't believe they're married. I have to hand it to them; they went for it. How did I miss it all these years? I know I was away a lot, but I always thought they were just the best of friends. I figured Finn was content spending his life in his garden. How could I have thought that would be enough?"

He looked at India. He hadn't meant to suggest anything. She smiled at him as they slowly swung their clasped hands between them.

"I'm not offended. Finn told me just the other night not to mistake my career for companionship. He admitted that he'd made that mistake himself. Not in so many words, but I can see now that's what he meant." She looked at him again. "That's not what I'm doing, Wyatt. I just want to be sure. I want that for both of us, and the only way to be certain is to get some perspective. And that only comes from time apart."

They walked in silence for a few minutes until they saw the lights of Woodshed.

"I don't want to talk about time apart yet, India. I plan to spend the next ten hours very much together."

He picked up the pace, pulling her toward the porch.

She laughed nervously, trying to keep up with him.

She had just unlocked the door when he spun her around, his face unreadable in the shadows, but his desire for her tangible nonetheless.

Wyatt grabbed her by the waist and pressed her up against the side of the building. He reached down, pulling her dress up high on her legs, his hands powerful and demanding on her thighs. She gasped when she felt his thumbs graze her underwear.

India grabbed the back of his head, crushing her mouth to his, her inability to get close enough to him driving her wild.

They kissed as if it were the last time they'd be allowed to. He knew exactly what he was doing to her with his hands, and it drove him crazy to feel her body respond to his touch so viscerally. He sent her over the edge, her ability to form rational thoughts shattered.

She couldn't get enough, even more turned on now that he'd begun to scratch the itch. She jumped up and wrapped her legs around his waist. Wyatt carried her to the door, then through it, and into the living room.

They stumbled together, in a frantic rush of peeled clothing, over to the couch. Wyatt won the race, ridding himself of his clothing in record time, available to help her do the same. The fire was crackling in the hearth, as it had been every evening she'd returned to her room.

Wyatt lifted her dress over her head and hesitated only a moment to admire her flawless beauty in the firelight before he sat down on the couch, pulling her on top of him, her legs straddling his as she sat down and took him in completely, their faces just inches apart.

He groaned at the pleasure of being inside her, a sound she felt to her core. They were as close as two people could be, and the sensation was unforgettable.

He knew he would never love like this again; she felt the same. They moved together, their bodies and souls in perfect harmony as he whispered to her, things that made her blush. Things that made her lose her mind. She knew the only way she could hold on to her sanity was to try to take back some control.

She bit him along his neck and sucked at his earlobe, knowing full well she was taking him to the edge when he quickened the pace again, his hands grasping her bottom, grinding her fully against him. Her hands reached back behind her and she grazed his inner thighs with her fingernails, hearing the sharp intake of his breath. But it wasn't until they'd reached the summit and suddenly stopped moving, looking into each other's eyes in complete stillness, that they crashed into each other so powerfully, they had to hold on for dear life.

There was nothing left to say. They spent the rest of that night letting their bodies do the talking. Sleep never occurred to them.

The sun rose much too quickly that next morning.

CHAPTER
TWENTY-SEVEN

They'd gotten up at seven and started the coffeepot, moving out to the screened-in porch to spend their last few moments together. Wyatt was sitting on the day bed, and India snuggled against him, nestled between his legs, her cheek against his chest. He'd wrapped the comforter from the bed around them both, keeping the morning chill at bay. Wyatt held her tightly, stroking her back, as she let her fingers trail through the hair on his chest.

He leaned down to kiss her forehead, his hands smoothing her hair.

"No matter what, I'll be grateful for this week I've had with you for the rest of my life."

India couldn't lift her head to look at him. She could feel his heartbeat, and she felt her own chest tighten at his words. She didn't want to leave him. They'd made love all night until they lay weak, and now she could feel her resolve slipping away. What if she didn't leave? She had a feeling that she could be fulfilled in a way she'd never been if she could just stay with Wyatt. She'd accomplished so much in her career, and it had never given her the peace that being with this man did.

And that terrified her.

She'd carefully planned out her life, and it had worked, for the most part, up until this week.

She hadn't seen this coming.

She wondered if this was how her parents had felt. Her mother had been a bit of a gypsy. She'd traveled all over the world with a backpack as her only companion for most of her late teens and early twenties. She'd found temporary work in each new city, making enough money to see what she wanted to see, before moving on to a new place or experience.

She'd told India how she'd met her father in an ashram in the Panchagiri Hills, where they'd both traveled for a self-development program. They were young, and it was love at first sight. Her mother told her they'd become so intertwined with each other during those early days that they'd almost completely surrendered their own individual identities. She'd gotten pregnant with India right away but didn't realize it at first.

They'd left the ashram, traveling around Europe after that, before coming home to the States. It wasn't long after her mother revealed she was expecting that India's father decided he didn't want to be a parent. It wasn't part of his journey, he said. He left, only returning briefly for the birth of his daughter and staying long enough to name her. They never saw him or heard from him again after that.

India knew that she, and her name, served as a constant reminder of everything that her mother had sacrificed. Her mother's depression was born the same day as her only child. She'd mourned her freedom for the rest of her life.

Now, India wondered if she was making the same mistake. She felt consumed by Wyatt, finding it impossible to get clarity while she was with him. She knew that she would regret not giving herself the chance to be absolutely sure before making a decision that could alter the course of her life forever. She would never let herself end up like her mother.

She didn't love him any less. She was just choosing to love herself too. She owed them both absolute clarity.

India reached up and stroked his cheek. Looking into his eyes, she didn't need to say anything at all. They could feel the love between them now, unspoken.

This kiss was different. There was an urgency, a desperation. She felt his need for her and reached down to caress him.

He inhaled at her touch, sure he would never get enough. He scooped her up off the day bed and carried her inside, the comforter still wrapped around both of them.

Wyatt set her down on the edge of the bed, India sitting up to face him. He stood before her, gazing into her eyes for a moment, before claiming her mouth. The taste of her was everything to him, and he worked hard to memorize the sensation of her hands on his body. An hour without her would be difficult. Weeks would be excruciating. He hoped she'd find it just as impossible.

He had one final thought as he fit inside her, watching her face recognize their union. He knew what it was to feel happy again, and she had been responsible for giving him that gift. He loved her infinitely in that moment.

❦

Violet and Rex had just finished breakfast when they heard the soft knock on the door. Sadie was still asleep, so Violet tiptoed across the room and turned the handle quietly. What she saw was heartbreaking.

India and Wyatt were standing on the porch, unaware of her presence. The look they were exchanging was wistful, their hands clasped together as they waited for her. Wyatt was pale, and it looked like neither of them had slept for days.

She cleared her throat to get their attention.

"I'm glad you came to say good-bye," she told India, opening the screen door to let them in.

They turned to Violet.

"Oh, we didn't hear you," India said. "I wanted to stop by and wish you guys safe travels, and to say thank you for everything. This week has been incredible."

Violet reached out and pulled India into an embrace. Wyatt felt even sicker than he had already, the knot in his stomach growing by the minute. He moved around the women, heading into the kitchen to stand with Rex to give them a moment.

"It's been our pleasure getting to know you, India. I hope you'll be back . . . sooner than later. I can't help thinking that you belong here, somehow." Violet gave her a sad smile. "But I guess that's for you to decide," she added.

India wiped the tears from her eyes.

"I don't want to hurt him, Violet. I just need to be sure. But I want you to know how much I love him. He's the most incredible person I've ever known. Thank you for being such a good friend to him."

Wyatt had helped himself to a glass of water in the kitchen and was staring out the window at the fog lingering over the meadow. Rex clapped him on the shoulder.

"You OK, man? I know this can't be easy."

Wyatt shook his head, at a loss for words. Rex poured himself more coffee and leaned back against the counter.

"She'll be back. I'm no psychic, but even I can see that what y'all have is special. Give her the space to realize it for herself. Have faith, brother."

Wyatt knew Rex was right. Their time was up, and all Wyatt had now was faith. He hoped it was enough.

They had just finished loading India's luggage into Olive when they saw Susan and Finn walking toward them, hand in hand, from the direction of the garden.

"We didn't want to miss our chance to say good-bye," Finn said as they got closer. "Besides, my wife needed to come out and give me a few ideas about how to do things better in my gardens. Day one and she's already nagging me."

Susan laughed, nudging him as she let go of his hand to walk toward India, taking the girl's hands into her own.

"I'm so glad to have met you, my dear. I hope you enjoyed your time here with us."

Susan smiled at the two of them, trying hard to ignore the devastated look on Wyatt's face.

"I'll look forward to seeing you in New York in a couple of weeks. Finn and I are making a honeymoon out of it when we come in for the interview. I do hope you'll be doing it?"

Susan kissed India on the cheek, reaching over and squeezing Wyatt's hand in the process. India smiled and collected herself.

"I'm so glad to hear that you're both coming. I am doing the interview; they sent me a text with the details this morning. I'll look forward to seeing you both. And thank you. For everything."

India turned toward Wyatt.

"But most of all for raising this man. He's remarkable."

She reached up and gave him a tender kiss.

Finn smiled in agreement. "He's alright once you get to know him," he joked.

They laughed together before the four of them hugged and said their good-byes.

Wyatt helped her into the truck one last time, taking a deep breath as he walked around to his side. It would be the fastest trip to the airport he'd ever known.

The terminal was busy as he pulled up alongside the curb. Wyatt made sure India's luggage was taken care of by the sky-cap before turning to meet her gaze. He struggled to say the words he'd been preparing for this moment.

She could see that he was fighting back emotion; she'd lost her own battle. Tears streamed down her face as she looked at this man she'd fallen so deeply in love with. She reached up, kissing him one last time. It was Wyatt who pulled back, taking her hands in his.

"I won't call you, but I can't promise that I won't be thinking of you every moment." He took a ragged breath and said what he knew he had to. "Please don't call me unless you're absolutely sure you want to be with me. I don't know if I can handle anything less than that. Know that I love you, India. More than any man has ever loved any woman. But I want you to be happy, and if being in New York makes you happier, then I'm going to have to accept that. I would never ask you to give up your career. But my life is in Tennessee, at least for the next year, and who knows after that? So I'm going to do what Rex suggested to me this morning. I'm going to have faith in us. But I'll always be here, loving you, no matter what."

He reached up to wipe her tears away. They looked into each other's eyes for a moment longer.

She kissed him good-bye then, turning to walk into the terminal while she still had the strength to do so.

CHAPTER
TWENTY-EIGHT

It had been much harder to leave than India had thought it would be. She'd had to physically restrain herself from running back out to him, watching from just inside the sliding doors as he'd stood there for a moment before turning to get into his truck. The look on his face broke her heart, because he looked like she felt.

Devastated.

It had only been a week, but her entire universe had shifted on its axis, and everything felt different now.

She barely remembered the flight home, staring out the window of the plane the entire way, reliving every second of their time together. The flight was bumpy, but instead of worrying about it the way she normally would have, she cranked up her music and thought about him.

Alanis Morissette suggested they'd be simple together.

If only.

India hadn't even realized they'd landed until someone tapped her on the shoulder.

"Honey, he must really be something. I haven't seen anyone that distracted in a long time."

The flight attendant flashed a smile at India, but as India turned toward her, the woman could see that whatever she'd been thinking about was also causing her pain.

"Do you need any help, sweetie?"

India shook her head and stood to gather her bags.

"No . . . thank you. I'm OK. I mean . . . I will be. I'm just ready to go home."

Which wasn't exactly true. She couldn't have explained why, but New York felt like the opposite of home to her now.

Her first week back at work had been awful. She wasn't sleeping well to begin with, her dreams fraught with nightmares. In one recurring nightmare, India was stuck on a steep trail, and Wyatt was on the edge of a cliff just above her. He was reaching out for her, begging her to take his hand. No matter how many ways she tried, she couldn't quite reach. Every time she'd get close, he would disappear, leaving her standing there alone in the woods. She'd wake up drenched in sweat, her pillow soaked with tears.

India had grown accustomed to the peace and quiet of Tennessee, so it was difficult for her to reenter the hive of humanity called Manhattan. Even her apartment felt strange now. She'd always loved the soaring windows in her living room, overlooking the Guggenheim and Central Park, believing they'd somehow brought the outdoors in. Now she realized it was all relative. What had once felt like welcome green space was now a sad and suffocating substitute. She missed the tang of wood smoke and the solitude of the mornings on the porch. Her bed seemed enormous, his absence like a chasm on the other side.

She'd always loved running in the city, but even that simple pleasure had inexplicably changed. The sidewalks seemed to confine her, and she found it hard to find a rhythm, even though she'd taken to running at night when she couldn't sleep. She'd stop and look up at the sky, hoping that at least it would look the same, the thought of Wyatt under the same blanket of stars bringing her small comfort.

But there were no stars in the city, the lights and pollution and buildings keeping them at bay.

At work, her colleagues welcomed her back, but she could tell that, even though the network had stepped up and invited her back, the small seed that Jack had planted was enough to take root in the fertile minds of her fellow journalists.

People questioned how exactly she and Jack had happened to be at the same resort at the same time, and she couldn't bring herself to put forth the effort to convince them that it was purely coincidental. And so, the question remained unanswered, her coworkers drawing their own conclusions. India was going through the motions, and it didn't take long for her bosses to notice.

A week after she got back, they'd called her in to the executive offices for a meeting. After chastising her for her rather lackluster performance, they reminded her of the upcoming piece on Blackberry Farm. The interviews were scheduled for the following day in Studio B, and she would indeed be conducting them herself. India was stunned to hear that it was happening so soon. She'd thought it was on the schedule for the following week. She felt her pulse quicken.

"Who's coming from Blackberry Farm . . . is it Susan Eden?" She found herself hoping that there might be a last-minute replacement. Someone . . . newer to the staff. Perhaps a photographer?

Stanley Ruff, the president of the news department, confirmed that it was indeed Susan.

"We're very lucky, though. She's bringing her new husband with her, who I'm sure you know happens to be the master gardener. We'd like you to interview both of them for the piece."

India smiled, trying to ignore the disappointment she felt. Of course he wouldn't come.

"That's great. I'm glad they're both available; they're lovely people, and Finn Janssen will make for great television. He's very smart but very folksy. They've both been at the farm for over forty years. What a win for us."

She stood to go, but then turned back toward her boss.

"Thanks for doing this piece, Stan. You saved my behind, but it's also going to be a really solid story."

Stanley waved his hand.

"Don't mention it, kid. I've been in this business a long time. And I've known Jack Sterling since he was still wet behind the ears. This nonsense will all blow over; you'll see. Viewers have very short memories. It's how we're able to recycle so many stories and make them new again. Turns out, there really isn't more than one way to skin a cat, but we can make people think there is with a new hook and some smoke and mirrors."

India stared at him. In that moment, he'd managed to trivialize everything she'd worked so hard for and believed in for so long. It was the ugly underbelly of the business. Then again, maybe she was just being sensitive.

"Thank again, Stan," she said, moving toward the door. He stood up from behind his desk.

"Oh, and, India? We need to get that interview about you and Jack on the schedule as well. The tell-all you promised us? Once you fill in all the details viewers have been clamoring for, it will definitely help put the rumors to rest. Let's plan on having you do a sit-down with one of the anchors next week."

India felt nauseous. She'd assumed the network would want to avoid any further mention of Jack, but they were obviously amenable if it stood to give them a ratings bump. It was hard to imagine a scenario in which she could come out of this with a shred of her dignity intact. She'd sold her soul to the devil, all right.

India agreed, smiling meekly as she left Stan's office, and closed the door behind her.

🍓

Wyatt was frustrated with himself for being so weak. He'd managed to make it eight days without succumbing to the temptation of finding a television set so he could catch a glimpse of her. He knew it would just make things worse, but every morning it was a struggle not to allow himself that small consolation. Since she'd gone, he'd tried and failed a thousand times to take his mind off her.

He couldn't outrun her. He'd need a new pair of shoes by next week if he kept up his current pace. On every trail, she was right there beside him, her memory woven into every passing landmark. The Yallerhammer. The fishing shack. Even the hiking trails were unexpected reminders of her.

Wyatt had offered to take Violet, Rex, and Sadie to the airport a few days earlier, not realizing the emotions that little field trip would trigger. He'd driven away afterward feeling like he'd been punched in the gut once more. He didn't care to ever set foot in that terminal again.

He'd tried working in the garden, but the sight of Woodshed was almost more than he could bear, and Finn knew it. The day before he and Susan left for New York, he'd assigned Wyatt an errand that he knew would take him off the farm the next morning, giving him some breathing space to clear his head.

Wyatt was at the counter of the hardware store in Knoxville, reaching for his wallet to pay for the supplies Finn had requested, when he glanced up and his heart skipped a beat.

She was even more beautiful than he'd remembered. He must have had an odd look on his face, because the cashier looked up when he didn't answer a question and followed his gaze to the television. Her eyes got big and round.

"Oh goodness, I've been waiting for this segment to come on! It's the owners of Blackberry Farm! On the *Today* show! Do you mind if I watch this real quick?"

She waited for Wyatt to answer, but he couldn't, so he just shook his head. He couldn't take his eyes off her.

She grabbed the remote, turning up the volume so they could hear the interview that was already in progress. Finn was saying something about how he and Susan were honeymooning in New York, when he suddenly grabbed at his chest, leaning forward off his stool and collapsing onto the floor. Susan gasped and scrambled down beside him, crying his name over and over. India somehow managed to collect herself, her stunned face drained of all color.

"We're going to take a break. We'll be back in a moment," she managed to say before rushing across the floor to where Susan was now covering Finn's motionless form.

The television went black, and a local commercial popped up, bleating about a furniture sale of some kind. The hardware store was eerily quiet, the few people who had gathered around to watch standing together in stunned silence. Wyatt couldn't understand what had just happened.

He grabbed his keys off the counter and sprinted out the door to his truck. He drove directly to the airport, praying he'd be able to get a flight.

CHAPTER
TWENTY-NINE

Susan stayed by Finn's side as the ambulance prepared to rush him to Mount Sinai on the west side of town. India promised she would get in touch with Wyatt, but Susan asked her to please wait until they knew more about Finn's condition. India reluctantly agreed, but she was conflicted. She knew Wyatt would want to be there to support his family. She decided that she had to tell him, but when she tried to call, his phone rang four times before going to voice mail. She decided to call the farm to see if they knew how to reach him. They didn't but promised to deliver her message.

Thankfully, her coanchors were still in the building, so they were asked to finish out the remaining segments of the show since India was too visibly shaken to go back on the air.

She'd told Susan as the ambulance prepared to pull away that she would meet her at the hospital but that she needed to make sure her shift was covered before leaving. The fear on

Susan's face made India's blood run cold. Finn was still lying pale and unconscious next to her, surrounded by the paramedics in the rig. India watched as they closed the back doors in a hurry and the ambulance screeched down the street and out of sight. She wrapped her arms around herself and rushed back into the building.

Stanley Ruff had immediately come downstairs after seeing the drama unfold live on the television from his office, and he found India gathering up her belongings, ready to leave for Mount Sinai. He blew out a breath, strangely thrilled about the events that had just transpired.

Any attempt to contain his excitement was thinly disguised, and he was wringing his hands in obvious delight. He grasped India on the shoulder as she was about to walk out the door.

"If you're planning to go to the hospital, I hope you'll make sure to secure a follow-up interview? The viewers are going crazy, wondering what's happening. That was incredible live television! I'll expect to see you back here tomorrow morning with a full report for our first segment. They might want something for the evening news too, so make sure to check in with us later."

India didn't speak. She couldn't, afraid of what she might say. She rushed out the door and headed to the hospital with a foul taste in her mouth the whole way.

🍓

Wyatt cursed the traffic. He'd made great time driving through Virginia and Maryland but found himself at a standstill a few miles west of Allentown, Pennsylvania.

He'd arrived at the Knoxville airport just after the morning flight to New York had departed, and couldn't imagine waiting seven hours for the next plane to leave, especially since thunderstorms in the area were threatening delays. He couldn't risk a cancelled flight, so he'd driven as far as he could before stopping to gas up, where he'd grabbed two large black coffees along with several maps. He was pissed that he'd left his cell phone at the hardware store and didn't have Google Maps at his disposal.

The station attendant was kind enough to lend him a phone, which he used to call the farm to find out if anyone had information on where Finn had been taken. The staff at the front desk said they'd heard from India a couple of times and that Finn was still in surgery, but they hadn't gotten any other updates in the past hour or so.

So India had called. He'd wondered if she would try his cell phone, and he kicked himself again for having left in such a rush. He needed to keep a cool head, to be ready for whatever Susan needed when he arrived. He prayed that Finn could hold on, for both of their sakes. He couldn't think about himself or India right now. He needed to focus on getting to New York as quickly as possible.

India and Susan huddled together in the family waiting area for most of the afternoon. It had been nine hours since Finn had collapsed on set, but it may as well have been nine days. Minutes felt like hours as they waited for news while the surgeons worked hard to save his life. Finally, just before seven in the evening, the automatic doors opened with a whoosh, and Finn's surgeon appeared like a mirage in the desert. Susan grabbed India's hand as they both rushed to their feet.

"You have a very tough husband, ma'am," he said, pushing the mask down below his chin.

"The surgery went well, but Mr. Janssen did suffer a heart attack. We were able to perform a triple bypass, and from the looks of things, he's doing very well. He only suffered minimal damage, so we expect him to make a full recovery. We're taking him up to the ICU recovery area now. I'll let you know when you can see him."

Susan clasped her hand over her mouth, finally letting the tears flow. India had marveled at how strong she'd been all afternoon, and seeing her vulnerability now made her appreciate this remarkable woman even more. Susan embraced the doctor, thanking him profusely. When he left them, she turned to India, tears still brimming in her eyes.

"Thank you for being here for me today. I was terrified that we were going to lose him, and I honestly can't imagine my life without that stubborn mule."

She wiped her tears, her resolve seeming to strengthen right before India's eyes.

"I suppose I should call Wyatt now. I couldn't bear the thought of calling him with bad news. I'm so glad I don't have to."

India reached over and stopped her from dialing. She gave Susan a sheepish smile.

"I've already been trying to call him all day; I know you asked me not to, but I knew it was because you couldn't tell him yourself. He's not answering his phone for some reason, but I know he's been checking in at the farm. I've been leaving word at the front desk, and they said he's called in a couple of times to find out what's going on. I'll call again now to tell them the good news."

India gave Susan a squeeze before walking down the hall to find a quiet place to make the call.

The elevator doors opened, and Wyatt found himself standing face-to-face with her.

"Susan! How is he? Is he out of surgery yet?" Wyatt pulled her into his arms and hugged her tightly.

Susan hugged him back, so grateful to see him there.

"He made it through OK, Wyatt. He's going to be OK. Oh God, I was so scared, but he's going to be just fine."

She pulled back to look at his face. He was clearly exhausted.

"Why haven't you been answering your phone? How did you get here so fast? We've been trying to reach you all day."

Susan looked around for India, but the hallways were empty. She led Wyatt back to the family waiting area.

Wyatt reached up, dragging his hands through his hair, and then stretched his back.

"I couldn't get a flight, so I drove straight here. I was at the hardware store when I saw you on TV. Scared the shit out of me. I took off so fast, I left my cell phone sitting on the counter. I've been stopping to check in at the farm every time I got gas. I guess they've been getting regular updates."

He glanced around the waiting room, wondering where India was. Susan grabbed his hand.

"India's been here with me all day. She just went to call the farm to give them another update, but I'm sure she'll be back any minute. I couldn't have done it without her, Wyatt. I can see why you love her so much."

Wyatt cleared his throat and looked out the window.

Down the hall, India had just finished up her call when Finn's surgeon rounded the corner.

"Miss Evans, I can take you and Mrs. Janssen up to see Mr. Janssen now. He's doing well and might be waking up soon. I'm sure he'd love to see you both there."

They started walking down the hall, but India stopped short.

She could see Susan talking to Wyatt in the waiting area. He was running his hands through his hair, his face darkened by several days' worth of whiskers. She had the sudden urge to run to him, but she stopped herself. In that instant, she knew. But she wasn't ready to see him yet. Not like this. Not here.

"Why don't you take Mrs. Janssen up with Finn's son, Wyatt? He's just arrived. Please tell them I'll see them later, but I'm afraid I have to go now. Thank you, Doctor."

She turned and headed for the set of elevators at the other end of the floor.

By the time Wyatt came looking for her, the hallway was empty.

CHAPTER
THIRTY

Susan and Wyatt spent the next few hours at Finn's bedside, leaving only to use the restroom or take turns getting coffee. Finn opened his eyes shortly after they'd arrived and recognized them right away, squeezing each of their hands. Doctors had taken him off the ventilator, which had made him much more comfortable. He was getting his color back and starting to look like himself again, and they were relieved when doctors confirmed that he was on his way to a lengthy but full recovery.

Wyatt intended on staying the night at the hospital, but Susan insisted he check in to the hotel for the evening to rest up after his long drive. She'd managed to finagle a private room for Finn in the ICU and was determined to sleep on the pullout sofa herself, insisting there wasn't enough room for both of them. She walked Wyatt out into the hallway, the two of them embracing just outside Finn's room. Susan put her hands on his arms.

"We have a room at the Carlyle, at Seventy-Sixth and Madison. I've already called over and reserved you a room too, so they're expecting you. Get some sleep, Wyatt. He's going to be resting all night anyway, and you'll be yourself again when you see him in the morning."

She placed her hand on his cheek, unable to ignore the pain in his eyes any longer.

"She's giving you space, Wyatt. I'm sure she'll be here to see Finn tomorrow. The two of you can talk then."

Susan leaned in and kissed him on the cheek before turning to head back into Finn's room. Wyatt stood there for a moment, debating whether or not to hang around the hospital in case India returned that evening. He decided that if she'd chosen to avoid him once already, it was probably better if he made himself scarce to avoid any awkwardness.

Walking out of the hospital, he couldn't help but wonder what the people at the fancy hotel would think when he pulled up to check in to their five-star hotel, leaving Olive behind with the valet.

He was glad he'd had the presence of mind to stop at the hospital gift shop first, considering he'd left home without so much as a toothbrush. He purchased the few things he would need to get cleaned up and then grabbed a change of clothes in the Carlyle's shop, which they'd kindly opened up for him after hours when he'd arrived.

He rode the elevator to the seventh floor, wondering the entire time why India hadn't at least said hello at the hospital. He'd just pulled the keycard from the lock, pushing the door to his room open with his knee, when he felt the weight of it pull away from him.

India was standing inside, her eyes soberly locked on to his.

He froze for a moment before stepping inside, letting the door slam behind him. He saw her flinch at the sound and instinctively dropped the bags he'd had in his hands, closing the gap between them in two broad steps.

She pulled him against her, and they embraced, holding each other for a length of time. When he lifted his face to hers, they both had tears in their eyes, his brimming with questions for her. She answered him with her kiss. Her hands caressed his face as she softly ran her tongue along his bottom lip before taking full possession of his mouth. He groaned at the taste of her, not needing answers now.

He walked her backward until her knees hit the bed, clipping her legs out from under her, the weight of his body on hers a welcome sensation. They fit together perfectly, each of them wondering how they'd survived the past nine days. He loved her then, with everything he was made of, letting his body tell her just how much. She felt cherished, cared for, safe. He was her true north, and it had taken her feeling lost to find him again.

Nothing else mattered when he slid inside her, the two of them connected, body, mind, and spirit. They moved together, slowly at first, then with urgency, never taking their eyes off one another. When they reached the peak together, they knew that neither of them could live without the other. The rest of it was just details.

They lay in each other's arms afterward, Wyatt running his fingers through her hair, her head on his chest. She knew she had some explaining to do. But first she wanted to know about Finn.

"Were you able to see Finn? I know how much that must have meant to both him and Susan that you managed to get here so quickly." She tilted her head so she could see his face.

He looked down at her and nodded. "He woke up for just a minute, but he knew we were there. The doctors said he'll be more alert in the morning, so Susan convinced me to come here to get some sleep."

He kissed her on the forehead and chuckled.

"I'm pretty sure this is the opposite of what she had in mind, but I've actually never felt better."

India smiled.

"I know you weren't expecting to see me here. I saw you in the hospital with Susan, and it took everything I had not to go to you then."

He scooted back against the headboard so he could see her better, and she adjusted so she was lying on her side, propped up on her elbow looking at him. Wyatt looked confused.

"Why didn't you, then? I knew you'd been there, but I thought you left because you didn't want to see me. I didn't understand why you would do that."

India closed her eyes briefly, then looked right at him.

"I knew we had so much to say to each other, and I wanted you to have that time with Susan and Finn. They needed you in that moment. I figured I'd waited this long, so what was a couple more hours? Turns out it was agony. I called Susan to find out a good time to come back, and she suggested I meet you here. She put my name on the room reservation. That's how I got in. So I think she actually might have had this in mind. But what took you so long to get here?"

Wyatt chuckled.

"Well, seeing as I left home with nothing but the clothes on my back, I had a couple of stops to make. That's what's in those bags I threw to the floor when I saw you." They laughed together before Wyatt grew serious again.

"What does this mean, India? Are you here because of what happened to Finn? Or are you here for me?" His stomach clenched as he waited for her response.

She sat up to face him, wrapping the sheet around herself. Taking a deep breath, she said, "I don't know what I thought would happen when I left you. I can tell you, it was a thousand times worse than anything I could have imagined. Loving you has changed me, Wyatt, and I can't seem to find my way back to my old self. The thing is . . . I don't want to go back. The life I left here two weeks ago isn't the one I returned to, and I know that's because of you."

She scooted closer to him, taking his hand in hers.

"It's like when you get a massage and you don't know you have lower back pain until someone starts digging around? Meeting you, and loving you, showed me what I've been missing. My job was great, until it wasn't. I don't want to do it anymore. I forgot how much I love photography, and I've been spending a lot of time writing this week since I've been back. Maybe that's what's next for me. Or maybe it's something I haven't even discovered yet. Who knows?"

She brought his hand to her lips as he sat up to face her.

"I do know one thing. It's not that I can't live without you. I'm choosing not to. I'm ready for all of the adventures that life has in store for the two of us. I can't imagine taking another trip around the sun without you." She leaned in to kiss him just to the side of his mouth, then the other side. Wyatt pulled back with wonder in his eyes.

"What are you saying, India? Am I hearing this right?"

She smiled, kissing him square on the lips this time. She leaned in to whisper in his ear, "I'm asking you to take me home, Wyatt. With you. Take me home to Walland."

EPILOGUE

Three seasons passed at Blackberry Farm, and India and Wyatt soon found themselves on the other side of a year. Spring brought new life once again, and as dawn broke that late-April day, they knew they were in for treat. The weeks leading up to that morning had been particularly warm, encouraging everything to bloom a little ahead of schedule. The meadows were filled with wildflowers, and the trees were budding, pregnant with the possibility of summer days ahead.

Now, as the late-afternoon sun streamed through the windows, India was sitting at the vanity in Woodshed, where she'd stayed the night before. Violet was standing behind her, braiding small pieces of her hair and pinning them back with sprigs of lily of the valley. Sadie was twirling around in her little pink dress, thrilled to be a part of the festivities and happy her parents had brought her back to East Tennessee after a year away. Violet and Rex's book was newly submitted to their publisher, having already gotten rave reviews from the people editing it, so the travel had been well worth it, but they were just glad to be home in Knoxville, especially for this day. It was exciting to think that this time next year, they could find themselves the proud authors of a bestselling book.

There was a knock on the door, and then Susan entered with a bottle of champagne in one hand and an envelope in the other. She smiled at the scene before her, grateful for these special people in her life. She handed the envelope to India and set about opening the champagne.

"I wanted us to have a moment to share a toast before the day gets away from us."

She popped the cork on the Veuve Clicquot, pouring four glasses. She pulled a fifth glass from the cabinet and poured an apple juice for Sadie. Handing out the glasses, she stood before them still holding two for herself. India looked at her, puzzled.

"What's with the second glass?"

She was just about to tease Susan about being such a lush, when the screen door opened again, and a nine-month-pregnant Julia waddled in, a huge smile on her face.

"Give me that champagne. I'll do anything to get this baby out of me, and I've heard that bubbles do the trick. Hopefully we're not too far to the hospital."

She rushed over to hug India, the two of them bursting into simultaneous laughter and tears.

"I thought you weren't coming . . . doctor's orders! What are you doing here, Jules?"

India rubbed Julia's giant belly, in awe that her friend could still look so beautiful this full of a baby.

"He said I couldn't fly. There was no mention of driving. So nine delightful hours in a car, and presto! Here we are! I shipped Mike off to be with the groom; I hope that's OK?"

India beamed at her friend. She couldn't believe she'd come all this way to share in their big day. She raised her glass to the incredible women in front of her.

"A toast to all of you. You're so special to me, and I'm so very grateful to have each of you in my life. To friendship, family, and, always . . . to love."

Wyatt had been warned that his wedding day would go by in a blur and that it would be impossible to remember every detail. But there was one moment he knew he would never forget.

The sun was setting behind India when she arrived at the boathouse on Finn's arm. He could make out her silhouette as she walked toward him, but it was only as she got close enough for him to see the look in her eyes that he'd come undone. He'd never felt love for anyone the way he loved India, and he knew she felt it too. He hadn't believed his good fortune when she'd agreed to be his wife.

They'd been on a hike together in the fall, the ring burning a hole in his pocket on the way up the mountain. He was terrified that he would lose it, so he'd kept his hand in his pocket the entire way. When they'd reached the top, she'd noticed that he'd stopped talking, and when she turned around, he was down on one knee. It was the same spot where he'd saved her from the bear. And she'd realized in that moment it was also the very spot that she'd dreamt about the week after she first left Blackberry Farm, where she'd been unable to reach him. This time, there was no trouble at all. He'd slipped the ring onto her finger, and she'd known in her soul that she would never be alone again.

They knew they'd always have a home as long as they were with each other. They'd loved spending the last year together in Walland, and Finn and Susan had made sure they knew that Blackberry Farm would always be an option to them.

Ever since Finn's heart attack, he and Susan had both had to make adjustments.

Once he was back on his feet, Finn had reluctantly admitted that the physical work of farming was behind him now, so he'd agreed to interview candidates for the head gardener position. In a happy twist of fate, Garrett, the bellman who had helped India on her first day, emerged as the most qualified. His grandparents had taught him a great deal about heirloom farming back in Washington State, so Finn knew he was the perfect fit for Blackberry Farm.

Susan wanted to have the freedom to travel more now that Finn was well, and she knew that if she remained in her role as proprietress, it would limit them. To that end, she'd drafted a letter and had given copies of it to both India and Wyatt just before the ceremony, naming them the new coproprietors. It was up to them going forward to manage things—or to hire managers as they saw fit, if they wished to have more flexibility themselves. Either way, they were the future of Blackberry Farm, and together they would make it great, however they chose to go about it.

Now, as they stood together in front of their family and friends, looking into each other's eyes, the future seemed limitless. Wyatt grabbed India's hands, fighting the urge to kiss his bride before being told to do so. She looked like a goddess. Her off-the-shoulder antique lace dress had a bohemian vibe that suited her. She wore her hair mostly loose, with a few flowers, and her cheeks had the blush of their first moments together. The image of her standing before him on their wedding day would be forever seared into his brain.

India's heart raced as she gazed at Wyatt standing across from her in his heather-gray three-piece suit, the white shirt unbuttoned at his throat, so quintessentially Wyatt. His face had the faintest hint of whiskers, and she blushed when she realized she was having wedding-night fantasies before the ceremony was even over.

Her voice was choked with emotion as she said her vows.

"Wyatt, you swept me off my feet from the moment I met you, and while that first week was white hot, this past year has made me understand the value of a slow burn. You're my constant, my best friend, and my partner in all things. I promise that I will love you, honor you, challenge you, and console you. When you laugh, I'll delight in the sound; when you cry, I'll be there to wipe away your tears. There is no one I'd rather spend the rest of my days with than you, and I'm honored that you feel the same way. I love you to the moon and back, and I can't wait to start the rest of our lives together, now, in this moment."

Wyatt smiled at her, giving the lump in his throat a moment to clear. He squeezed her hands as he spoke.

"India, waking up each day next to you is such a gift. Your positive attitude and your love for life are contagious. You are kind to everyone, and my family and friends love you like their own. I'm humbled by your thoughtfulness, whether it's as simple as making me a cup of coffee, pulling back the covers for me to join you in our bed, or the way you looked after Finn and Susan when they needed you most. You're the light of my life, and I can't wait to write the next chapter of our incredible story. Thank you for loving me so completely. I promise that there will never be a night when your head hits the pillow without knowing how much I cherish you and the life that we are building together. I love you with all my heart. Thank you for marrying me."

With those words, Wyatt finally kissed his wife.

They'd spent the year before their wedding building a home together up on the ridge. The house was incredible, with huge windows that made it feel like they were living in a tree house. They talked often of filling it with children one day, but not yet. They wanted to enjoy some time alone together first.

They didn't spend their first night as husband and wife in that new house, though.

After their reception in the Yallerhammer, they walked hand in hand under the stars, past the chapel. As they came up the gravel road, they could see the twinkling lights hanging off the awning of the Airstream. Wyatt turned to India, his face young and happy.

"Welcome home, Mrs. Hinch." He swung her up into his arms and carried his wife inside.

ABOUT THE AUTHOR

© Terri Carrick

Andrea Thome is a former broadcast journalist, having covered both sports and news during her career. She currently lives in Chicago with her husband (a retired professional baseball player) and their two children. She spends her spare time traveling and pursuing her other passion, photography. You can see a sampling of her photography and learn more about *Walland* at www.andreathome.net. *Walland* is her first novel. She is currently working on the second book in this three-book Hesse Creek Series.